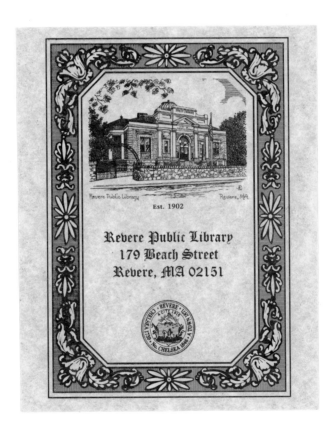

Est. 1902

Revere Public Library
179 Beach Street
Revere, MA 02151

CHEYENNE PASS

Center Point
Large Print

Also by Lauran Paine and available from
Center Point Large Print:

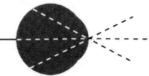

**This Large Print Book carries the
Seal of Approval of N.A.V.H.**

CHEYENNE PASS

Lauran Paine

CENTER POINT LARGE PRINT
THORNDIKE, MAINE

This Circle Ⓥ Western is published by
Center Point Large Print in the year 2019 in
co-operation with Golden West Literary Agency.

First Edition
October 2019

Printed in the United States of America
on permanent paper.
Set in 16-point Times New Roman type.

ISBN: 978-1-64358-371-6

The Library of Congress has cataloged this record
under Library of Congress Control Number: 2019945576

CHAPTER ONE

The sheriff was a young man, with all the physical bloom and all the confidence of young men. He sat his horse straight up, his clear eyes drifting from that sharp rise he and his companion stood upon, out over the endless run of countryside.

He was medium in height but thick and sturdy. His face was good, the lips long, the chin solid, the eyes steady and fearless. There were a few little squint wrinkles at the outer corners of those eyes, but otherwise the sheriff's face was almost boyishly smooth.

All around lay a broken country of sage-purpled hills, tilted, grassy meadows, and farther back the dark heights of pine-timbered mountainsides. There were meadows down among those rolling sagebrush hills. There were also cottonwood trees, indicating ample, shallow sub-surface water.

Southward lay a particular valley; it was long and narrow and appeared to end—as it actually did—against the distant flanks of a raw-boned rampart which ran east and west, cutting off its continuing southward flow of grassy flatness. There was a town down there. In morning's golden summertime brightness that town seemed small, huddled, and dingy.

For a while the young sheriff sat there gazing at

that town. Beside him, the older, more weathered man, atop his muscled-up, big, black horse, also viewed that town. But this older man had lived so long that there was now no vitality to his gaze. He was loose and easy where the young sheriff was upright and tightly wound.

The older man looked east and he looked west. Where they sat was the only visible pathway through this rugged mountainous, broken country. There was a road down below them a few hundred yards. It came straining up out of that big valley where the huddled town lay, straight as an arrow. Then it achieved this eminence, ran perhaps a half mile along in a dead-level way, and dipped again, heading steadily northward through interminable twists and turns, sometimes clinging precariously to a side-hill, sometimes plunging down into some gloomy cañon. But that road never stopped, and as far as one could see from up in the pass, there was no other comparable road anywhere about.

There were some little crooked feeder roads heading toward that town down there, but there were no other genuine thoroughfares heading northward, and this was exactly why the sheriff and his companion were sitting their horses now.

"One way in," said the quiet, loose-seeming, older man, "and one way out." He fished around in a vest pocket, found his tobacco sack, and went to work casually twisting up a smoke. "I thought I'd run across every game folks play to make money, but this is a new one on me."

The younger man, Sheriff John Klinger, blew off a big sigh, looped his reins, and scratched his head. It was hot up in Cheyenne Pass this time of year. Hot and sometimes dusty, when one of those unaccountable little vagrant breezes came along, and lonely.

"It's ridiculous!" exclaimed Klinger, watching his deputy light up and expansively inhale. "No one in his right mind would block a road."

The older man's pleasant, candid face twisted into a tough little grin. "The problem is," he said quietly, "that no one's sure who's in his right mind and who isn't. When Richard DeFore says he owns something, he isn't bluffing and he doesn't consider himself crazy by a long sight."

"That's for the courts to decide," snapped the youthful lawman. "All I know right now is that if he tries to have one of the stages stopped for passing through here, he's going to think he grabbed a lion by the tail."

Deputy Sheriff Ethan MacCallister canted a skeptical eye at Sheriff Klinger, wagged his head slightly, and said: "Too bad your first month in office you had to run into something like this. You know, John, when I used to be sheriff, about the only trouble we had was from some occasional drunk cowboy . . . or maybe some fly-

7

by-night gambler drifted in, got roughed up, then got locked up."

Sheriff Klinger frowned, turned, and put a smoky gaze upon his deputy. "Why'd you take the job? I mean, during the campaign I wasn't very flattering to you."

MacCallister chuckled. "Oh that," he murmured. "Why that didn't much bother me. In politics when you run against someone, you're sort of expected to run them down. Wouldn't hardly do for a fellow to say his opponent was a good man. Men don't get elected to office saying things like that."

"But why, Ethan?"

The older man stared far out through narrowed, faded eyes. For a long time he didn't answer. But ultimately he said: "Well, John, you're a good man. Young maybe. Inexperienced. A mite hot-headed and over-zealous perhaps. But at your age I wasn't much different." Ethan stumped out his cigarette on the saddle horn, tossed it away, and added: "I wanted to see you get started on the right foot, I guess. But aside from that . . . what else can an ex-sheriff do for a living when he gets to be my age . . . work in a livery barn, swamp out the saloons?" MacCallister shook his head, and he was no longer smiling. "Naw, he just steps down. Becomes a deputy instead of a sheriff."

"Well, whatever your reasons, I want you to

know I'm grateful, Ethan. And about those things I said during the campaign . . ."

"Forget 'em. Four years from now you'll run again and someone else will most likely be accusing you of worse things. It's in the game. If every defeated politician stayed mad over what his opponent said about him, this whole country would be full of soreheads."

The sheriff returned his attention southward for a time, then drifted it off onto their right and left. After a while, he said: "No sign of DeFore's riders. I'm beginning to think this whole thing was just a bluff."

MacCallister didn't think that at all. "Never underestimate a man like Richard DeFore," he admonished. "I've known DeFore since you were in knee pants. I've never yet known him to make a bluff."

"We haven't seen any patrolling riders up here."

"That's true. But when he said from now on anyone crossing his land had to pay a toll, he meant it. And if we haven't seen any DeFore men yet, that only means they've seen us first and are lying low."

"What time is it?" the sheriff asked, shooting a slit-eyed look at the climbing sun.

"About ten. The stage'll be along directly. Damned thing is never on time anyway."

Sheriff Klinger lowered his face and looked

9

down his nose at the empty, dusty old stage road. "Danged old fool," he growled, obviously meaning Richard DeFore. "Who's he think he is anyway? Cheyenne Pass has been an open road ever since the Army built it during the Indian wars."

"It's across his land, John."

"Well hell, all roads are across someone's land, aren't they?"

"Originally, sure. But folks sell right of way, or they donate 'em. DeFore swears he never did either one of those things."

Klinger gestured with an angry fist. "What else could this dog-goned pass be used for, but a road?"

"Nothing," placidly agreed his deputy. "But that's not the point."

The sheriff dropped his hand, became suddenly stiff in the saddle, and after a moment of long study, he said: "Here comes the stage, straight northward out of town." The sheriff lifted his reins. "We better get down on the road."

The two of them reversed their horses, cat-footed it down off their vantage peak to the twisted, broken, hilly country below, and went zig-zagging easterly toward the place where eastward and westward hill-sides fell back, making a natural pathway through this up-ended country.

That oncoming coach they'd seen had been a considerable distance off. In fact, it was still down the far side of Cheyenne Pass a couple of miles, so there was no great hurry. Still, Sheriff Klinger pushed his animal right along, breaking out of a sage stand to impatiently strike the roadway and halt.

Deputy Sheriff MacCallister didn't make his horse go through the spiny sage at all. He took his time, came out a hundred yards northward, then walked his mount down where Klinger was waiting.

Looking around with his dark scowl, the sheriff said: "Where are they? DeFore said he'd have men up here. Well, if he wasn't running a bluff, where are they?"

MacCallister also scanned the surrounding hills, peaks, and gloomy little arroyos that opened out upon the southward roadway which was under their observation.

He said: "Don't worry, they'll be here." He made that pronouncement as a man speaks who has unshakable belief in what another man has said.

And soon they were. Six horsemen dropped down off a brushy hill a quarter mile ahead, on the west side of the pass, riding loosely and confidently. They were facing Sheriff Klinger and Deputy MacCallister for a hundred yards before they had to swing westerly and complete their descent, strike the edge of the road, and halt there.

Klinger's nostrils flared. His face darkened. "They looked straight at us," he said. "They saw us plain as day, Ethan."

"Sure they did. Those boys have their orders. You don't have to talk to 'em to see they're set to do exactly what DeFore has ordered them to do."

"They won't do it!" exclaimed Klinger, and started forward.

MacCallister considered Klinger's sun-bronzed, iron-set profile and also urged out his animal, trying to explain: "John, there are times when being a live squaw is a lot better than being a dead buck."

Klinger didn't seem to hear. He was concentrating his full attention upon those six riders up ahead, and those cowboys were in turn sitting insolently over there, returning that dark look.

"John," said MacCallister, "you better calm down. It's not up to us to interpret the law . . . only preserve the peace. Until the courts have had a chance to say whether DeFore's got the right to close this road or not, your job's not to force any fights."

Klinger looked fiercely around. "DeFore's got no right to stop that stage."

"No? If this is his land and there's no existing right of way across it, who's to say he can't turn it back?"

"I say so!" the sheriff insisted.

"John, you can't make that decision. That's why we got law courts. You go forcing a fight now, and when the smoke clears, if you're still alive, you damned well might be in more trouble than Richard DeFore will be in."

Suddenly the sheriff hauled back, stopping his horse. They were still well beyond earshot of those six men down the road who were sitting their saddles like they were carved of stone, watching the pair of law officers.

"Then what is the law supposed to do in this mess?" demanded Sheriff Klinger, his face sweat-shiny and rusty colored with hot blood. "Let him turn that coach back?"

"Yes. That's exactly what *our* kind of law is supposed to do."

"Consarn it . . ."

"Listen, when you accused me of being too easy as sheriff of Sherman County, you didn't know what you were talking about. I never said that of you during the campaign, but I'm telling you now because you got the job. You don't know the first thing about being a sheriff! You draw your gun against those DeFore riders now, and they'll have every right under the sun to kill you . . . and I'm betting they'll do it too. *You'll* be at fault, *they* won't. A man's got a right to defend his life even against the law, if the law's wrong, and right now you're dead wrong. They can turn that stage back. I've been trying to drill that into your stubborn skull for hours now. They can turn it back. You can't do anything until the courts decide whether you're right or DeFore's right, and you've got to sit back and await that decision!"

CHAPTER TWO

Sheriff John Klinger's expression slowly and stubbornly turned troubled. He looked from Deputy MacCallister on down the road where DeFore's men were sitting. They looked back, particularly Richard DeFore's ranch foreman, Travis Browne, who was obviously the leader of those six men.

Browne had no reason to like John Klinger. They had known one another four years, since both had arrived in the Cheyenne Pass country with a herd of Texas cattle. At one time they'd been friends. But that had been before Ruth married Klinger. After that had happened, Browne never again spoke to John.

Browne had been very much in love with Ruth. So had John. It was not a new story and the result was inevitably as it always must be. Ruth had to decide which man she would marry. She had chosen John, and a friendship that had been under great strain all the time both men were courting her, abruptly disintegrated.

But there had been another complication to that marriage. When Klinger had asked MacCallister, while they sat their horses atop that little peak, why he hadn't lambasted Klinger during the recent election campaign, MacCallister had

15

skirted all around the real reason why he hadn't. Ruth MacCallister was his daughter. She and Klinger had been married even then. How could a father, whose only child was blindly in love with his opponent in the election, say anything against that opponent?

He couldn't, and MacCallister, realizing this, had not really campaigned for re-election, so he'd lost and now he was not only the deputy of the man who'd beaten him, he was also the new sheriff's father-in-law. And actually, these were the true reasons he'd swallowed his pride and taken the deputy's job under Klinger. The fact that Ruth had come to him in private and begged him to help her husband, and keep him from being killed, was known only to Ruth and Ethan MacCallister. They had always been close, but even if they hadn't been, Ethan still probably would have taken the deputy's job, for, as he'd said, what is there for ex-sheriffs to do. They know only lawman work.

So now, as they watched DeFore's riders, and were in turn watched by them, they sat ten feet apart with their somewhat divergent, private thoughts, and meanwhile that oncoming stage made its approaching dust and noise, bringing them constantly closer to crisis.

Klinger sat stiffly, uncompromising, but the undiluted determination of shortly before seemed, after what Ethan had told him, less virulent, less likely to provoke violence.

MacCallister, on the other hand, sat easy in his saddle, and it was now upon his craggy, weathered countenance that those six men down the road concentrated. They didn't fear the former sheriff, they didn't fear any man, but they mightily respected MacCallister and not just for his fast gun, either. MacCallister, like their boss, was a man who never bluffed, never spoke hastily, and he was slow to make judgement. When Ethan MacCallister appeared somewhere, like now, he meant business, so those DeFore cowboys waited and watched and spoke quietly back and forth among themselves.

If they meant to back down, they didn't have much time left to do it in. That oncoming coach was now less than a quarter mile off and would soon come dusting it up over the top out bearing northerly through Cheyenne Pass.

Browne, a solidly built, curly headed, dark-eyed man of Texas, squared around in his saddle with obvious determination. He looked southward, awaiting the stage's appearance. It was abundantly clear to everyone—his own men as well as those two mounted lawmen sitting a hundred yards north—that Browne would stop the stage.

And he did.

When the coach broke out over the last little

rise, came heavily lurching along trailing its gray-dun banner of pulverized dust, Browne raised his right hand, made a forward motion sending his five hard-looking riders across the road in a solid, closed-up rank. As Browne dropped his arm, he threw a long, appraising look up toward the lawmen, before urging his mount forward as the stage groaned down to a rattling halt.

The driver and shotgun guard, sitting atop their high seat, said nothing at all. They simply sat there, watching Browne and his men blocking their onward way. Occasionally, they sent a sidelong glance at the two motionless lawmen farther out. Clearly, both driver and guard had been expecting this. Clearly too, they'd both received instructions about how to act. For neither of them spoke nor touched their weapons. For that matter, neither showed any expression at all, except a wooden watchfulness.

Browne rode down to the coach's side, halted, put a solemn gaze upward at the two men on the high seat, and said to the driver: "Clem, turn it around and head back . . . or pay a two-dollar toll fee."

The driver was a small and wiry man with calm, fearless eyes and a look of capability to him despite his slightness. He was perhaps thirty years of age but, because of his smallness, seemed younger. Like all the men in that roadway, he knew Browne and all the others within his sight.

He shook his head gently. "Can't pay the fee," he said, and it sounded as though he was repeating something he'd been told to say. "If I did that, Travis, it'd be establishin' a precedent, and the company manager down in town says we can't do that."

"Then I guess you turn around and head back, Clem," Browne advised him.

But the stage driver made no move to lift his lines. Instead, he gazed solemnly up where the sheriff and deputy were sitting.

"How about it?" he called to those two.

Klinger's hand visibly tightened on his reins. He eased his animal forward at a slow walk. MacCallister rode along beside him and stopped when Klinger did, ten feet behind that line of silent DeFore men blocking the road.

This was the moment they were all awaiting, particularly Clem and his companion perched upon the stagecoach's high seat, for they'd known down in town that Klinger and MacCallister would be up here when this confrontation occurred.

Down the coach's side a rickety door opened and a man got out. He was dressed in the small-brimmed hat, the long frock coat, and the polished boots of a town-dweller. But there was something about this man that put the others in mind of leashed violence.

He was tall, slightly over six feet tall in fact,

and he was whittled down to rawhide toughness. Those fancy clothes did not conceal anything about him. Particularly, they did not conceal the chilling fact that he wore two ivory-butted six-guns belted around his middle and lashed to his legs. His face was bronzed and it was set in an expression of scorn. He stood there beside the coach facing that full roadway of mounted men, looking from either side of his high-bridged, hawk-like nose at them. His eyes were pale, spaced wide, and as hard as wet iron.

"You," this stranger said to Browne, "move your men out of the way."

For an interval of surprised silence no one moved or spoke. Every eye was upon that tall, shiny-booted stranger. Men of his obvious calling were anything but rare in Colorado, but with the possible exception of the stage driver and the shotgun guard, not a one of those men, including Sheriff Klinger and Deputy MacCallister, had expected to have a professional gunfighter step out of the coach.

They all sat still, looking but saying nothing.

The stranger reached up, thumbed back his narrow-brimmed hat. He then made a practiced backward sweep with both elbows clearing his coat away from those matched .45s he wore. He gave the lawmen and DeFore's men a challenging look, both his hands hanging within three inches of his ivory-butted Peacemakers.

20

"Mister," he said, again addressing Browne, "I told you to clear your riders from in front of this coach."

The DeFore range boss eased forward slightly in his saddle as he continued to regard the two-gun man. He slowly turned his head, threw a look up where Clem sat, gave his head a little sardonic wag, and looked on out where John Klinger and Ethan MacCallister sat.

To the lawmen he quietly said: "One's too old, one's too green . . . so they bring in a professional."

Browne's meaning was clear. He was impugning the courage and the ability of the sheriff and his deputy.

Klinger's face darkened at Browne's insult, but when he spoke, it was to the tall gunfighter.

"Mister, stay out of this. I don't know who hired you and I don't care . . . just stay out of this."

The gunfighter raised one eyebrow. "I don't think I can, Sheriff. You see, I'm an employee of the stage line, too, and my job's simply to protect company property from highwaymen."

"These men aren't highwaymen," stated John Klinger, "but, even if they were, it's the law's job to . . ."

"Sheriff, I'd say they *were* highwaymen," broke in the gunfighter, his sulphurous gaze steadying upon Klinger. "They stopped this coach. They're armed and they're obviously bent on interfering with the established operation of the stage line. Furthermore, this is a public road and . . ."

"Shut up, stranger," MacCallister barked. Up until the minute he said that, he had been ignored by the others. "Move your hands clear of those guns," he instructed.

Browne, Clem the driver, even Sheriff Klinger swung astonished looks at the deputy. MacCallister was making fight talk and this was a very bad time to do that because not a one of those men was a professional, except the two-gun man, and while the odds might be greatly against the gunfighter, the rest of them were fully exposed should a fight commence.

Then MacCallister moved his right hand the slightest bit and the others saw why the former sheriff was making his fight talk. While Browne and the gunfighter had been warily considering one another moments before, and while MacCallister himself was unobserved, the deputy had drawn his right-handed .45. The solitary black snout of that gun now lay lightly over Ethan's saddle swell, bearing straight upon the chest of the two-gun man.

The gunfighter saw that pistol barrel but he did not immediately obey the deputy. Instead, he ran a slow look from the tilted muzzle on up to MacCallister's face.

For about ten breathless seconds those two steadily and silently regarded one another.

Then the gunfighter gently let his arms come forward, let his frock coat drop back down, once again concealing the ivory butts of his guns, and he said without any trace of amusement: "Deputy, you took a long chance, and for nothing. This doesn't change anything."

MacCallister's slitted eyes never wavered, never blinked. "Mister, get in the coach," he ordered, "and enjoy the ride back to town. I won't disarm you. I don't believe you're the sniping kind. Just climb back up into that coach, sit back, and take in the scenery."

The deputy raised his eyes a little, his tone of voice remaining soft and commanding as he told the stage driver: "Clem, it's time to turn the coach around and head on back to town."

The driver wrinkled his nose at MacCallister and Sheriff Klinger. "Which side you boys on?" he asked.

"Not on the side of an outfit who'd do what your company just tried," answered MacCallister. "Gunfighters aren't the answer, Clem. You tell Hank Weaver at the stage office I said that, too. You tell him we'll be along to see him when we get back to town. Now turn the coach and head on back."

Clem leaned out to peer around and down where the gunfighter still stood. Clem's physical movement was the thing which seemed to break all that stiff tension. Travis Browne's riders still blocking the road shifted in their saddles, looked gravely at one another, then on over to where Browne was again sardonically gazing at the tall, well-dressed professional gunman.

"Mister, don't buy in," Browne warned the gunfighter. "This is a sort of private feud. If the stage line imports gunmen, my boss will no doubt find it necessary to import some." Browne drifted his look up to Clem. "You tell Hank Weaver he's a damned fool for trying this. Mister DeFore'll hear about it."

Clem was blushing. He seemed uncomfortable and embarrassed as he gathered his lines and said a trifle sharply to the two-gun man: "All right, mister, get in like the deputy said, and we'll head back."

The gunfighter ignored Clem for a moment. He kept studying Ethan MacCallister, still with one eyebrow slightly raised, still with those wet-iron eyes of his with their look of controlled violence. Finally though, he turned, grasped the door, started to step up, but paused to say over to MacCallister: "Deputy, you're kind of old for making damned fool plays like that. Next time I'll know you. Next time you won't even clear leather with that gun of yours."

Clem whistled at his horses. Browne's riders broke away left and right to allow the stage teams to make their big roundabout turn. Slowly the stagecoach went out, around, and returned to the roadway, southward bound.

While the others were thoughtfully watching all this, Sheriff Klinger leaned over and said: "Ethan, you were the only one who kept his head."

Watching the coach, MacCallister made a short answer. "That damned fool of a Hank Weaver . . . sending a gunfighter up to force a passage?"

"He almost did it," observed Klinger.

"No, he didn't. Travis was making up his mind to fight. If Weaver had had a lick of sense, he'd have sent three or four. Then Travis wouldn't have tried it. But sending just that one man . . . hell, there's no six range riders on earth who'd ever let one danged gunfighter back them down. All Weaver did was come close to provoking a battle. That's what happens when store clerks and their kind start playing at being strategists."

Browne ran a slow, flinty look over where the sheriff sat with his deputy, saying nothing, not even giving the men a nod. Instead, he jerked his head at the DeFore riders and led them eastward off the roadway and back into the rugged hills the way they had come down.

None of those cowboys looked back. Klinger and MacCallister sat there as alone now as they'd been two hours earlier when they'd been atop their little vantage point waiting to see what was going to come of old Richard DeFore's fierce ultimatum that from now on Cheyenne Pass was his private toll road.

"Let's go home," MacCallister announced, and started riding down through the gray-dun cloud of dust the stagecoach had left in its wake.

CHAPTER THREE

The town of Winchester had once had another name, but that had been a number of years earlier when it had been established as a supply depot for the Army during those interminable punitive expeditions against the Indians, and there weren't many folks still around who even recalled that name now.

Winchester lay in its rich, long valley with mountains all around it, seemingly dependent upon the north-south roadway for survival. But actually there were a number of big cow outfits in the hills, some ore mines, and even a little logging to make up the bulk of Winchester's economy.

Most of its buildings were less than twenty years old, but some, like the log jailhouse, which had been an Army post stockade, the livery barn, which had been a big mess hall, and the only log saloon in town, which had been the officers' quarters, were left over from those earlier times when the whole place had been an Army town.

The jailhouse was huge, built of enormous logs set one atop the other, notched at the ends, and stoutly chinked. It had steel-barred windows and an oaken door, iron-bound and thick enough to withstand anything but the direct hit of a cannonball. It had been built for strength and for no other purpose. In summertime it was like an oven. A man standing and considering it from any angle would deem it massively ugly. But in some scarcely definable way it seemed to point up, by its very forbidding exterior, the might and determination of the law.

When Sheriff Klinger and MacCallister got back to Winchester from Cheyenne Pass and sent word they wanted to see Hank Weaver, the local stage manager, at the jailhouse, Weaver came at once. The law around Winchester commanded that kind of respect.

Weaver was a bean pole of a man with a nervous tic—he batted his eyes when he was under stress. He was getting bald and this, coupled with his perpetual look of astonishment, sometimes put folks in mind of a startled crane when they looked at him.

Weaver entered the office where Sheriff Klinger was waiting. He shot a look past him to Ethan MacCallister, with whom he'd been friends since both were in their twenties. Weaver batted his eyes.

Klinger gave Weaver no chance at all. He said roughly: "What in the devil were you trying to do today, Hank? Whatever made you think sending that gunfighter up to the pass was going to do any good?"

Weaver stood uneasily by the door and looked

from one lawmen to the other. "Two weeks back," he explained, "when all this came up, I wrote the head office down in Denver. Yesterday, this gunfighter showed up in town with a letter from one of the bosses, which he gave to me. According to the letter, he had orders to break any deadlock which might exist up here."

"So you sent him up there today?" questioned Klinger.

"No, I didn't," contradicted Weaver. "He came by this morning when I was getting the coach ready, informed me no other passengers were to ride out this morning, got aboard, and told Clem to whip up the horses."

MacCallister was over by the gun rack, listening. Now he said: "Hank, you didn't give that fellow any orders at all?"

"You gotta understand," stated Weaver shrilly, "I have no authority to tell him anything. The Denver office sent him up here, and, if anything, he acts like he's the boss, not me. When he said no one else was to ride that coach, I had four people to make refunds to." Weaver emphatically shook his head at MacCallister. "I got no authority over that fellow at all, and I'll tell you something else, too . . . I don't want no authority over him. I've seen his kind before. I'm a peace-loving man. Gunfighters aren't my notion of the kind of folks I care to associate with."

"Where is he now?" asked John Klinger.

"Down at my office. He won't leave, just sits there, staring at me, smoking a big long cigar, and looking like the cat that just ate the canary."

Klinger twisted to look back at MacCallister. Clearly, the young sheriff didn't quite know what to do next.

MacCallister stepped away from the gun rack, strolled over to the stage-line manager, and said: "Hank, what's he waiting for?"

"An answer to that telegram he sent, I guess. I didn't ask him. As far as I'm concerned I wish he'd go sit somewhere else . . . in one of the saloons maybe, or over at his room in the hotel. He makes me plumb nervous . . . him and his fancy clothes and his dead-fish eyes."

"He sent a telegram?" the sheriff asked.

Weaver's eyes batted. His head bobbed up and down swiftly. "To the head office down in Denver. I'll tell you boys something. He didn't like it one little bit when you turned that coach back instead of letting it go on through."

The deputy made a wry little smile at Weaver. "That's not what he didn't like, Hank. He didn't like having someone get the drop on him. No gunman likes to be backed down in front of other folks."

Weaver's eyes widened. "You?" he said breathlessly. "Ethan, you threw down on him . . . and didn't get shot?" He stared at the deputy, then blew out a ragged breath and wanly shook his head. "You didn't recognize Ray Thorne . . . either of you! He's killed men from here to California."

Klinger and MacCallister exchanged a long look. "Ray Thorne," said the sheriff. "I've been hearing about him since I was a kid. Hank, is that what that letter said . . . that he was sure enough Ray Thorne?"

Weaver whipped his head up and down in strong confirmation. "Listen, Sheriff, do me a favor. Figure some quick way to get this right-of-way business settled. Or at least figure out some way to get Thorne out of Winchester . . . out of my stage office. Unless we can start sending the coaches out within the next few days, we might as well lock up the office and the barn. There won't be any business. And with him hanging around, folks are going to quit even coming in to pass the time of day. So do me a favor . . . get rid of him. Please." Weaver stood there wringing his hands, batting his eyes, and looking on the verge of tears.

The deputy sheriff responded with: "Thanks for coming down. We'll do what we can. See you later, Hank." He stepped past, opened the road-side door, and held it open until Weaver had departed. He turned back into the room, let out a sigh as he closed the door, tipped back his hat, and put a slowly gathering frown upon the sheriff.

"Ray Thorne here in Winchester," MacCallister said as if he couldn't believe it. "I remember hearing that like most gunfighters, he had a specialty. Some of them represent big cattle interests. Some do dirty work for the railroads. I once heard it casually said that Thorne is a stage-line specialist."

But Klinger wasn't thinking about the notorious gunman when he said: "DeFore will explode when he hears the stage company is ready to fight him over that damned road."

MacCallister watched his son-in-law pass across to their shared desk and drop dejectedly down in the chair behind it. The sheriff was finally beginning to appreciate the ramifications that accompanied that badge he wore.

The deputy sheriff was silent for a long time. Trouble had a way of sobering hot-bloods, of tempering them into what they afterward became, if they remained in law enforcement work—good lawmen. But there was nothing Ethan could do to expedite that process for his son-in-law and he knew it. All he could do was hope to guide Ruth's husband, which was exactly what he'd proposed to do from the day John had been elected sheriff of Sherman County. So he stood there now, studying the younger man's troubled expression, saying nothing.

After a while Klinger looked up and said: "Ethan, there's just one thing worse than making a mistake. That's refusing to admit that you made it in the first place."

"I'd agree with you on that," MacCallister commented.

"Well, I never should've run for sheriff. This morning, if you hadn't been there, I'd have forced a fight up in the pass."

"Oh hell," the former sheriff said. "It didn't come to a fight, and that's the important thing."

"I never should've run for sheriff. That was a mistake and I'm admitting it to you, Ethan."

A slight feeling of uneasiness began to firm up in MacCallister's mind. He was afraid what his son-in-law might say next, so he spoke up hastily, hoping to avert anything unpleasant between them. As a lifelong law enforcement officer, Ethan MacCallister didn't believe there were many occupations which equaled the lawman's profession.

"Listen, John," he said, "no one's born knowing exactly what to do in every situation. But sometimes men are born too stubborn to learn, and when that happens they're not going to be successful at anything. You aren't that bull-headed. This morning up in the pass you listened, and you acted about right. As for being sheriff . . . take my word for it, son . . . you're going to be one of the best this county ever had. I know. I been following this line of work all my grown-up life, and if there's one thing a fellow learns as sheriff, it's how to size up other men."

"But because we made the stage turn around and head back for town," Klinger stated forcefully, "DeFore will think that we're favoring him in his dispute over the right of way, and that's not the way it should be."

"No, he won't think any such a thing, John," MacCallister insisted. "I've known that old firebrand a long time. He'll know exactly why we did that . . . to avert bloodshed. And unless he's changed an awful lot this past year, he'll be grateful for us keeping the peace."

"Him," Klinger said, standing up and darkly scowling, "grateful? That dog-goned old cuss is meaner than a roiled up rattler even when he's in a good mood. I know. Remember I repped at his roundups before I got to be sheriff." The young lawman looked over at his father-in-law. "Ethan, you may have known him a lot longer than I have, but I know his kind. Every big cow outfit between here and the Cimarron has one like him. Opinionated, rough-talking, willing to fight, mean and powerful."

MacCallister stuck to his point of view. "You convince Dick DeFore he's wrong, and he'll back down."

"Yeah? And how do we do that?"

"I already told you, we let him have his day in court with the stage company and anyone else who challenges his right to exact a toll for going through the pass."

Klinger stared at his father-in-law and gently shook his head. "You know better, Ethan. You're just saying that. I'm not convinced it would have worked out that way before, but I know DeFore well enough to know it's sure not going to work out like that now . . . not after Travis Browne tells DeFore about Ray Thorne."

MacCallister privately agreed, but he would not say so. Instead, he said: "John, go on home to your wife and get something to eat. Tell Ruth I'll maybe drop by for a spell this evening. One thing's sure, there won't be anything else happening today. It'll take DeFore at least until tomorrow to get set for whatever he figures to do next."

Klinger's frown didn't abate even after he nodded and headed over to the door. He knew as well as MacCallister knew, that they hadn't settled anything between them, and that whatever was going to happen—while it probably wouldn't occur today as the deputy had just said—would very likely only be postponed until tomorrow. Still, MacCallister was right—or at least they both felt that he was—the sheriff might as well go home, enjoy his supper, and have a good night's rest. Worrying wasn't going to do any good.

After Klinger left, MacCallister went to the little woodstove, made a fire, put on a pot of coffee, and rolled and smoked a cigarette. He was indignant. For the first six months a new sheriff shouldn't have to handle anything but drunks, an occasional horse thief, or maybe a wife-beater. Whatever fate governed things like this had no business dumping a potential shooting war into his son-in-law's lap.

While he stared at the woodstove, the office door opened and a slight, wispy man entered. He closed the door, and looked owlishly over at MacCallister's craggy and resentful face.

" 'Afternoon, Ethan," the visitor said in a tentative manner, his hand still upon the door latch as though uncertain of a welcome.

"Hello, Clem. Sit down. I'll have coffee ready directly."

The stage driver advanced up to the chair, but he didn't sit. His face relaxed a little. He shot the woodstove a quick look as though verifying the fact that the coffee pot was indeed on, then he dropped down, hooked his thin arms over the back of the chair, and said: "I wanted to tell you that it wasn't my idea . . . what happened up in the pass today. When Thorne got in my coach, he told me what to do. I didn't have no say at all."

"Sure," MacCallister said easily. "I figured as much, Clem. You looked embarrassed when he jumped out of the coach up there."

Clem made a wry little grin. "Well, later maybe," he said, "but when Thorne first stepped

36

out, I was sweatin' pure lead. You know, a fellow up on a stage seat is pretty much exposed. I was tryin' to remember some prayers while Thorne was talkin'. I thought for sure Travis was goin' to make a play."

"He would have, Clem. He would have. Of course, Browne didn't know that it was Ray Thorne. But I'm not sure, even if he had known, that he would have let any man back him down in front of all of us."

Clem rested his chin upon the arms he'd crossed over the chair back, and steadily regarded the former sheriff for a moment. Then he said: "Ethan, Mister Thorne just give Hank orders to send the coach up there again tomorrow mornin'."

"And you think Weaver will do it?" said MacCallister.

Clem scratched his head, still carefully watching Ethan. "What choice does he have?"

"That damned fool's going to get himself killed, Clem."

"Well, if you're talkin' about Thorne, that's fine by me if he gets himself kilt. But right now I've got a different problem. The shotgun guard went to Hank after Thorne told him, and he quit. Said he'd be hanged before he'd go up to the pass again."

MacCallister, with the glimmering of an idea, said: "I see, Clem. So that leaves just you."

"Yeah, it sure does. Now what I come down here about, Ethan, is to ask if you'd ride up on the box with me tomorrow. You know I've got a wife and kids, and I got me a house here in town, so I can't just up and quit like the guard did. And I got the same bad feelin' about tryin' that twice, just like the guard did."

"And you figure if I'm up there on the box with you, maybe I can prevent a fight."

"Yeah, something like that. How about it, Ethan?"

"Does Weaver know you're asking this?"

"No." Clem straightened up and said a tart word. "Hank's so flustered by everything that's happened that you can't talk to him about anything."

"Let me think on it," MacCallister said, getting up and heading over to the stove.

"What is there to think about? You and John want to keep the peace. I'm here to tell you that if that coach goes back up there tomorrow with Ray Thorne on board, there's goin' to be serious trouble."

MacCallister poured two chipped crockery mugs full of black java, walked back, and handed a cup to the stage driver. "Be careful," he admonished, "it's hot."

Clem held the cup but didn't take his eyes off the deputy sheriff. "You gonna try evadin' this thing?" he asked pointedly.

MacCallister resumed his seat at the desk, sampled his coffee, found it scalding hot, and relaxed because that's how he liked it.

"You know better than to say a thing like that, Clem. But there's more to this than just riding the box with you tomorrow."

"Like what, I'd like to know."

The deputy took a sip, but screwed up his face when he realized the coffee was bitterly acidic. He paused before responding to Clem's question. "Well, like that stage not leaving Winchester," he finally said.

Clem stared and very gradually began to shake his head. "You'll never talk Hank into goin' along with that. He's too afraid of Thorne. And even if you could, you'd never get Thorne to call it off, and right now he's givin' the orders down at the office."

MacCallister said placidly: "We'll see about that, Clem. What time you figure to pull out in the morning?"

"Nine, like always."

"All right. I'll have an idea by then."

CHAPTER FOUR

In a town the size of Winchester when anything as unusual as a smoldering feud between the largest, richest cowman in the locality and the local stage line occurred, all the less important facets of existence swiftly fall into the background. The same applied to the active participants of such a feud, but once it became generally known that the fancily dressed dude with his matched ivory-butted six-guns was probably the most notorious and durable of that will-o'-the-wisp fraternity of gunfighters, Ray Thorne, local interest sharpened, saloon gossip became unusually lively, and every sporting man had a wager to make one way or the other.

There was no possible way to keep Thorne's identity from reaching Ethan MacCallister's daughter, so when Klinger went home that afternoon, following the confrontation up in Cheyenne Pass, he found his wife absent and a cold supper laid out for him on the kitchen table.

Ruth MacCallister Klinger, with a shawl over her shoulders, walked into the sheriff's office not ten minutes after Clem Whipple had departed. In fact, MacCallister was still sipping that original cup of hot coffee when his daughter came through the door.

He put aside the cup and smiled upward. "Hello, honey, John left about twenty minutes ago. He ought to be home by . . ."

She dismissed what he said with a wave of her hand.

"Dad, is that man the stage company sent up here really Ray Thorne, the gunfighter?" she asked, her hands shaking and her eyes wide in a fearful look.

Easing forward, MacCallister squared a chair around and motioned Ruth toward it, saying: "Honey, sit down and relax." He hadn't seen his daughter this agitated in a long time.

Ruth was a fair-complexioned, clear-eyed woman of twenty-five. She had curly blonde hair and a look of youth that made her seem four or five years younger than she actually was. It was difficult now, seeing those two in the same room alone, to note any marked resemblance, and in fact Ruth didn't much resemble her father. She was the cameo image of her mother, dead seven years now. And yet in her sturdy, solid build, she was like Ethan. Where she differed markedly from him, which perhaps had more to do with age than heritage, was in her manner now, for he sat there as calm, as imperturbable, as stone, while Ruth was anything but calm.

She took the chair and sat, but she did not relax

42

and her clear eyes clung to her father, awaiting his reply to her question.

He said quietly: "I reckon so, honey. I reckon that stranger is Ray Thorne. But that's nothing for you to get so upset about."

Ruth locked both hands across her stomach. "Nothing to get upset about!" she exclaimed. "Dad, my husband is the sheriff!"

"Well, sure he is, Ruthie, but Thorne's made no threats. In fact, we met him up in Cheyenne Pass this morning and sent him back to town."

"You and John did that?"

"Yes, honey. And he went right along. Now listen to me. As long as John is sheriff, he will be meeting up with the Ray Thornes of this country. I told you that when he decided to run for sheriff. I explained all the perils to you, honey. I also explained them to John." Ethan leaned back in his chair, considered his daughter for a thoughtful moment, before continuing. "You know, if your mother were here, she'd tell you being married to a lawman isn't the most secure life there is, but that after a while, if that's what your man wants from life, you learn to live with it. I reckon she'd also tell you that while there's danger, it's very seldom as bad as one's imagination can make it seem."

Ruth lost some of her stiffness under her father's quiet philosophizing. She leaned back in her chair, unlocked her clasped hands, taking in deep breaths. Finally, she said: "Dad, promise me you'll stay with him. That you won't let anything bad happen to him." She stopped, but then added: "Or you."

"Of course I'll stay with him. I promised you that when he was elected, didn't I?"

Ruth nodded. Her gaze turned misty. She got up, went over to kiss Ethan's leathery cheek, then she left.

For a full fifteen minutes after her departure, with outside shadows thickening, the former sheriff sat there, scarcely moving, as he reflected how Ruth was painfully like her mother had also been at twenty-five.

Finally, he left the jailhouse, strolled along the northward sidewalk in the balmy dusk, and paused in front of the stage office. The place was dark. He went on around to the back where the corrals and barn were, found several hostlers playing cards, and asked a few questions of these men before returning to the roadway again.

A few cowboys were beginning to drift into town as it was still early for Winchester's night life to start up, but that didn't prevent the exceptionally eager riders from hitting town for a few head-start beers, or perhaps a woman-cooked supper over at the hotel dining room or one of the town's eateries.

MacCallister considered the hotel for a moment while he teetered upon the plank walk's edge before coming to a decision. Thorne would perhaps be there. He was obviously a meticulous man who would prefer the amenities of a hotel over a boarding house. The deputy could picture him dressing carefully before a mirror in his Denver clothes of high quality, and he made a rueful face about that. None of the men around Winchester were fancy dressers, not even the ones like Richard DeFore who could've bought and sold a dozen Ray Thornes without missing the money.

He stepped down off the walkway into the roadway dust, crossed over, but as he stepped up onto the opposite walk, he turned northward and by-passed the hotel entrance entirely. He would meet the gunfighter tomorrow morning, for if he sought him out now, then the ensuing meeting would be pointless, and MacCallister, with an idea beginning to form in his mind, wanted that morning meeting to be the crucial one.

He strolled into the Teton Saloon, nodded at several idling men, crossed to the bar, and bought a drink of ale from Rusty Millam, night bartender and part owner in the Teton. MacCallister and Rusty had been friends for years. In fact, eight years before when Rusty had first come into the country, dead broke and hungry, it had been MacCallister who'd staked him and gotten him a job. Once Rusty had proved himself, it was MacCallister who made the loan necessary for

Millam to buy into the Teton. All those loans had long since been repaid, but the balance—due of goodwill—could never be repaid.

Rusty Millam was the warm, outgoing type of man never to forget that, so, while he served MacCallister his ale and picked up the coin that the deputy tossed down, Rusty leaned far over and spoke swiftly in a lowered voice.

"That Ray Thorne the stage company sent here from Denver has let it be known that if any DeFore men comes in here while he's drinking, he'll call 'em out."

MacCallister listened, drew back, and raised his glass. Over the rim of it, he said quietly: "Rusty, you got your shotgun under the bar loaded?" When Millam nodded, the deputy drank half of the ale from the glass, set it down hard, and said: "If he tries anything like that in here, Rusty, you use that scatter-gun."

The freckled, rusty-red-haired Millam, about thirty years of age, was thin and likeable and he had increased the Teton Saloon's trade considerably since buying into the place. But he had a definite rule about becoming involved in feuds like this one.

"I think it'd be better for me to side-step this one than mix into it, Ethan," he said, wrinkling his forehead as he placed a pained look of silent protest on the deputy. "One way . . . I could lose all the DeFore Ranch business. The other way

. . . I could wind up dead. You know that Ray Thorne's reputation . . . he's a killer. I wish to hell he'd decided to patronize some other saloon in town."

To this, MacCallister had nothing to say, so he finished his ale silently, turned away from the bar, and gazed out over the room. There were no DeFore Ranch men in sight but that didn't mean much. Richard DeFore's home ranch was six miles from Winchester. When his men rode into town for a night's revelry they invariably arrived late.

"Ethan?" MacCallister faced back around again, and watched Millam thoughtlessly wipe his bar top with a rank rag. "Is it true the stage is going to try the same run again tomorrow?" the saloonkeeper asked.

"That's what Clem told me, Rusty."

"Well, maybe you ought to know that Thorne isn't figuring on being the only one inside the coach this trip."

MacCallister regarded Millam stonily for a long while without uttering a sound. Around him, the room's noises ebbed and flowed. As newcomers walked in out of the darkening night they were greeted by acquaintances already waiting for the poker games and serious drinking to begin. The bar began to fill up, too, and Millam's assistant barman was kept busy while Rusty and the deputy sheriff stood across from one another

47

down where the bar turned and met the wall.

"Where'd you hear that?" MacCallister finally inquired.

"Eavesdropped on Thorne when he was in this afternoon. He was sounding out some of the boys. Heard him offer ten dollars gold just for riding up through the pass with him inside the coach."

"Did he get any takers?"

"Four," replied Millam soberly. "Strangers to me . . . looked like the usual run-of-the-mill unemployed riders on their way through town." Millam made a particularly wide sweep with his bar rag, leaned over, and whispered: "Two of 'em are sitting at that table behind you . . . near the door. Those two big, rough-looking fellows playing twenty-one. But don't turn now, they been watching us."

Finished cleaning the bar top, Millam turned and walked on down where the clamor for service was getting profanely loud.

For a minute or two MacCallister toyed with his glass. He returned an overly friendly greeting from some new arrivals to the saloon, then casually watched before heading toward the door. As he passed the table where the two range men were indifferently playing twenty-one, he threw a quick, sharp look downward. Both the men were strangers to him, and, as Rusty Millam had observed, they seemed to be another pair of unkempt, unemployed drifters, nothing more.

The deputy passed out into the warm night, spotted a light over at the stage office, and decided to head on over, stepping into the roadway and across the street. By now the saddle horse traffic was thicker as riders converged upon Winchester. It was also fully dark out. So dark in fact that when he walked into Hank Weaver's office, he had to pause a moment until his eyes grew accustomed to the pale light coming from the single lamp.

At the desk, Weaver was nervously shuffling through a wrinkled stack of papers. When he looked up and recognized his caller, Weaver put the papers down abruptly. His nervousness obvious, he tried to explain once again. "Ethan, I couldn't do a thing about it. I already told you, Thorne's got a letter of authority from the Denver office."

His eyes twitched as he grew more nervous watching the former sheriff walk over, lean upon the wooden counter, and put an appraising gaze upon him. When MacCallister said nothing, the stage-line manager blurted out: "I'm going to quit. I'm not going to have Denver send up a man like that to tell me what to do . . . not after I worked so hard for this company for twelve years. I'm going to quit and can't anyone talk me out of it."

Dryly, MacCallister said: "You need a drink, Hank." Then he fished around for his tobacco sack and cigarette papers. "Get hold of yourself. That coach isn't going to leave town tomorrow."

"What?" exclaimed the stage manager. "Not leave town. Thorne's already given the orders, Ethan."

"I don't care. It's staying right here in Winchester."

"You can't do that, Sheriff . . . I mean . . . Deputy. . . ."

"No? Who says so?" MacCallister asked as he lighted his smoke, exhaled a blue stream of smoke which he watched float toward the ceiling. When he shifted his eyes back to Weaver, he asked casually: "Why can't I, Hank?"

"W-Well . . . ," Weaver stammered.

Shifting his stance to get comfortable where he was leaning upon the counter, MacCallister pointed a finger at Weaver and said: "You're not saying I can't forbid the coach from leaving, are you? As far as Ray Thorne is concerned, I haven't seen anything of this letter of his saying he's now the boss here in Winchester. So, tomorrow morning that coach doesn't leave town."

Weaver's eyes blinked rapidly and shifted aimlessly around the room for some place to settle other than on the deputy sheriff.

He put the lawman in mind of a trapped wild animal, full of desperation and uncertainty, full of

50

a terrible dread of something he could anticipate but could not define.

"You don't have to tell Thorne his coach isn't leaving town," MacCallister said as he pushed up off the counter. "I'll take care of that when the time comes. You understand?"

"No," whispered the troubled stage-office manager candidly. "But I won't say anything to him, Ethan. Still I am going to quit . . . just as soon as Denver can get someone else up here."

"No, you're not," MacCallister said in a soothing voice. "You're too good a man for the stage company, but that doesn't mean you should quit. Besides, if you did, then Thorne's in charge for sure and you don't want that to happen do you?"

"No!"

"And that's why you're not quitting. Good night, Hank."

CHAPTER FIVE

Klinger was already at the office when MacCallister showed up a little later than usual the following morning. The younger man didn't look as though he'd slept well the night before. He was making coffee over at the woodstove when his father-in-law walked in, and immediately his face indicated he was relieved.

MacCallister noticed this and said: "You give me up for dead?"

Filling two cups with coffee, Klinger waited for MacCallister to settle in before he answered. "Ruth heard about what happened up in the pass yesterday . . . about Thorne. She was pretty worried."

"Yeah, I know," mumbled MacCallister as he picked up his cup, thinking about the state his daughter had been in last night when she had stopped in the office. "Sort of worried is right," he said as he took a sip, smiling before he added: "You know, that's one thing I just never can do . . . make decent coffee. So I just concentrate on making it hot."

They went over to the desk and stood a moment regarding each other. The sheriff put his coffee on the top of the desk, untouched, then said: "I heard about Thorne ordering the stage out

53

this morning." He waited for MacCallister to comment.

Instead of making any retort though, the deputy sheriff finished off his coffee, then drew forth a thick gold watch from his pocket, flipped it open, and gazed at the spidery black hands. He flipped it closed and pocketed it.

"Let's take a walk up to the stage office," he said. "I found out last night Thorne's hired a duo to ride along with him. Rough-looking, down-at-the-heel, bronc-stompers, from the looks of them."

Klinger's brows drew inward and downward at this unexpected revelation. "What do you aim to do . . . arrest the lot of them?"

"Maybe . . . maybe not. That depends on Thorne. But I'll tell you one thing we've got to do, John. Keep that coach from leaving Winchester, because if we don't, and if Thorne and his friends go up into the pass, this time there's going to be a fight."

"How long can we keep this up?" Klinger asked, getting more frustrated. "I mean, sooner or later Thorne's going to sneak out of town with a stage."

"Well, I wired the stage company's head office in Denver last night asking if they've appealed to the courts for a settlement of this feud. Should have an answer back in a day or two, I reckon, but until we do hear, we've got to keep on trying to delay things. So let's do that." MacCallister crossed to the door, opened it, and waited for his son-in-law to walk on out into the dazzling brightness of the summertime morning.

As Klinger brushed past, Ethan said: "At some point today, we've got to go see Dick DeFore. There are two sides to this mess. If we can delay 'em both a few days, I think the stage line will take DeFore to court. That's about the length of our implication so far."

Out on the plank walk, Klinger turned to look back at MacCallister, saying: "You sure got it all figured out like there's a simple way to handle this. I think different. I think Thorne's going to make a battle out of this. That's the only way his kind can keep drawing their big wages."

The two men walked northward with Winchester bustling in its usual fashion around them. They had very little more to say to one another until, with the stage office directly ahead, they saw Clem Whipple drive his coach out through the side road from around back and turn to bring the horses to a halt in front of the office, the customary procedure for loading passengers. Only this morning, there were no passengers in sight, except for the two rough-looking men standing under the overhanging roof in front of the office and idly looking over the town.

"That pair," said MacCallister, nodding his head in their direction, "Thorne's reinforcements."

"He's not particular when it comes to selecting friends, I see," the sheriff responded after running a narrowed look at the two. "If ever I saw a brace of mavericks, those two sure fit the description. Did you happen to get their names?"

"Didn't ask," MacCallister replied, shaking his head as he kept a close eye on the two. "Besides, if they take our advice and move on today, no one'll care what their names are. If they don't move on . . ." He let the words trail off as he lifted his burly shoulders and let them fall, his meaning amply clear.

Alone, Clem Whipple sat perched on the high seat of the stage. He slowly looped his lines upon the brake handle, throwing a worried look backward as he twisted to the left and right. Clem's face suddenly cleared when he saw the lawmen approaching. He sprang down with sudden alacrity as Hank Weaver walked stiffly out through the office door.

Weaver had on his usual green eye-shade and rumpled suit. He was even carrying the clipboard he always had in hand when the coaches were arriving or departing.

Force of habit, MacCallister thought to himself, studying Weaver. Out loud, he commented: "Why is it that some men, when their world starts falling apart, hang on to established rituals tighter than ever?"

"I assume you're talking about Hank," his son-in-law said. "In his case, I'd say it's just plain fear."

They were still a hundred feet south of the stage office when the immaculately attired two-gun man walked out onto the plank walk. Ray Thorne did not even glance in their direction, probably because as he emerged from the building his two hirelings drew themselves upright to catch his attention.

Both lawmen watched as Thorne said something to the two down-at-the-heel cowboys. MacCallister also noted that Clem and Weaver turned to gaze over where the three stage passengers stood talking.

Speaking softly but crisply, the former sheriff said: "I'll split off here, John. You walk on up and engage with Thorne."

"What are you going to do?" the sheriff asked.

"While they're all concentrating on you, I'm going to go around the far side of that coach and unhitch the wheelers."

"Be careful," Klinger advised.

When MacCallister was sure they weren't paying any attention to his movements, he stepped off the plank walk, angling wide enough so that the rear of Clem's coach ultimately hid him from the view of Thorne and the others in front of the stage-line office. He picked up his pace as soon as he saw that his son-in-law had become the focus of the group. MacCallister could hear everything being said once Klinger got up close and halted to address Thorne, but he couldn't see those men beyond the horses anymore.

Though he could not see who John was addressing specifically, he heard him say: "The stage isn't leaving town." A period of silence followed this announcement. MacCallister remained stock-still as he waited for a response. Finally, he heard Thorne's soft but lethal voice.

"Sheriff, you're beginning to get on my nerves. Unless you have a legal writ, just how do you figure to keep this stage from leaving?"

Working as fast as he could, MacCallister got the traces unhitched from the doubletrees behind the right-hand wheel horse when he heard his son-in-law say in that same sharp-edged tone: "Mister, I don't need a writ. Not to keep the peace. And I'm telling you this stage doesn't leave Winchester."

MacCallister worked his way over to reach for the hooks behind the left-hand wheel animal. From his new position, he happened to glance up. Clem Whipple was staring straight at him, the only man out of the group standing some twenty feet away, who was not concentrating his entire attention upon the sheriff. Clem's face was pale to the eyes as the deputy released the second set of chain harness tugs, leaving the horses unhitched to the stage except for their collar hitches. MacCallister eased back to work his way forward and complete his job at the same time Ray Thorne spoke up.

"That's not good enough, Sheriff. This here coach's going south for all you know, not north." Thorne paused, turned, and jerked his head sideways at his two hirelings. "Get aboard," he said.

Both cowboys started for the coach's side door. Clem now moved with a gray face but with solid resolve to block the doorway. One of the cowboys dropped his right hand and snarled at Clem.

The driver turned, gave the cowboy a stare, and said: "Either one of you fellows know how to tool a coach and four?"

This temporarily diverted everyone's attention. Even the gunfighter gazed over at Whipple.

"Driver, get up on your box," Thorne ordered impatiently. "Don't mix in where you've got no business."

MacCallister knew what Clem was doing and mentally thanked him. Clem's little respite had given him all the remaining time he'd needed. The stage horses, although they did not appear to realize it, were standing in front of their coach, but they were no longer harnessed to it.

The former sheriff stepped around the nigh lead horse, which put him fifteen feet behind the six men. At once the two cowboys saw him, but neither Ray Thorne nor Hank Weaver did.

They lost all interest in little Clem and steadily regarded MacCallister. That he was their enemy, that they recognized him as such, was plain in both their faces. But neither of them made a move toward the guns they wore because, exactly as MacCallister had done once before, he had drawn his six-gun unnoticed. He now stood flanking all of them with his gun up and ready.

When he cocked the gun though, this little grating sound warned Thorne. But it wasn't the gunfighter who moved. It was badly frightened and completely astonished Weaver. Thorne stood like stone caught between Sheriff Klinger in front and Deputy MacCallister behind. He was far too seasoned to buck odds like that, so he stood motionless with his narrow, fierce face turning steadily dark and wrathful.

Weaver whipped around at the sound of the six-gun being cocked behind him as though propelled by strings. He looked out of bulging eyes at the deputy and dropped his clipboard, his eyelids flicking.

"Easy," MacCallister warned. "Get out of the way, Hank."

The stage manager got out of the way, completely. He walked stiffly but rapidly back into the building behind them and did not re-emerge.

"Mister Thorne," MacCallister said, watching for even the slightest movement from the gunfighter, "you're not going anywhere." He paused, switching his attention to the stiffly standing cowboys, before saying: "You two . . . go get your horses and ride on out of town. Don't be in Winchester one hour from now or you'll get locked up for vagrancy." MacCallister jerked his head. "Get going!"

For several seconds the two cowboys glared at the deputy. They were not cowards, which was obvious, and they were angered at being ordered out of town like this. But neither, apparently, were they fools, which they would have had to have been to argue with the deputy's cocked six-gun.

The one with the longer hair seemed to lose the tension from his body first, then the other one also relaxed. They turned as one and, without a word or glance at the man who had hired them, went striding in the direction of the livery barn.

Not until then did Clem Whipple lose his rigidity and breathe evenly. Even John Klinger seemed to sense that there would not be any gunfire exchanged.

Thorne turned, hooked both thumbs in his black shell belt, and put a smoky look upon Ethan MacCallister. For a long while Thorne just stared, but ultimately he shared his assessment of the situation.

"I keep underestimating you, Deputy. This makes the second time you got the drop."

"Unless you leave town, too, Thorne, there'll likely be a third time."

Thorne shook his head at this and his meaning was very clear. "No third time, Deputy," he grated. "Next time, you'd better shoot whether you're in front of me or behind, like now, because I'm going to."

Klinger dropped his right hand as Thorne threatened his father-in-law. He was convinced the gunfighter was going to try and draw and fire. So was Clem. But MacCallister, giving Thorne stare for stare, surprised them both by gently shaking his head at the gunfighter.

"Draw if you're of a mind to," he said. "But the coach isn't leaving town even if you do, Thorne. You see, those horses are unhitched. They're just standing there out of habit. But you shoot a gun beside them, and in five seconds they'll be charging up the road, running free. Since they're the only team for that northward run . . . or even a southward one . . . and since I doubt like the devil you'd be able to fetch 'em back before nightfall . . . like I said, Thorne, the stage remains in town today."

For a full minute Ray Thorne kept regarding the deputy sheriff. Then he slowly turned, stepped to the plank walk's edge, looked down at those loosely hanging tugs, and let out a resigned sigh. He didn't seem so cold and angry now at all. In fact, when he faced about and looked over at MacCallister, his steely eyes were almost respectful.

"I wonder just how good you are with that gun," Thorne mused aloud. "You're clever, Deputy, I'll hand you that. But how many times can you come up with clever delays? What happens when you have to rely on that pistol?"

MacCallister put his head a little to one side. He'd known dozens of gunfighters in his time. Some were psychotic murderers, some were simply men who could not bear the thought of other men being better than they were in anything. Some, like two-gun Ray Thorne, were coldly calculating and icily efficient. They were the worst of the lot and certainly the most deadly.

"I'll tell you, Thorne," MacCallister said firmly. "If you keep trying to force a fight, you're going to find out about me and this gun. I'll tell you something else, too. I've been using this gun for over twenty-five years and I'm still above ground. You're not the first gunslinger I've had to tangle with. The ones I've met . . . well, they're all dead now and I helped plant my share of 'em."

Thorne nodded. He was not angry now. He was quietly calculating instead. He had known his share of lawmen, and while he did not say so, legend had it authoritatively that Ray Thorne had planted a number of them over the years.

"How do you want it, Thorne?" MacCallister

asked. "I can have Clem whip those horses up and chase 'em out of town, or I can save a lot of horse-hunting time if you'll agree that you've lost this round and that you'll stay in town today."

Thorne smiled with his lips but not with his eyes. He swung toward Sheriff Klinger and said: "I understand he's your father-in-law as well as your deputy. Well, Sheriff, I'm going to give you a piece of advice . . . fire him by tomorrow or I'll kill him."

Thorne turned on his heel, walked past Klinger, and struck out for the Teton Saloon across the way. He didn't walk fast and he never once turned to look back. He had said exactly what he intended to, and he was certain that none of those men who'd heard him had any doubt whatever that he was a man of his word.

Deputy Sheriff MacCallister leathered his weapon, wiped sweat off his forehead, then addressed the stagecoach driver and his son-in-law: "Clem, put up the coach and horses. John, let's go get our animals and ride on out. Thorne won't leave town but we've got to make damned sure nobody rides *into* town."

From his office window, Hank Weaver peered out. He was terrified. He had been unable to hear what had transpired and all he could do was watch the pair of lawmen stroll away and then sink into a chair weakly.

CHAPTER SIX

The telegrapher caught MacCallister at the livery barn where he and Klinger were saddling up. He had an answer for the lawmen from the stage company's head office down in Denver.

"Saw you coming over here to the barn," he said to the deputy, "and figured you'd be heading out, so I brought this over. It's the reply to that wire you sent."

MacCallister took the slip of paper, read it, carefully folded it before stuffing it into a shirt pocket. "Thanks, Al," he said to the telegrapher, and might have turned away except that the telegrapher pushed out a hand to shake, saying he hoped Ethan and John had a safe trip.

MacCallister, with his lifelong perceptive quickness, sensed something here. He reached out his hand, grasped the telegrapher's hand, and pumped it once. As soon as their palms met, the telegrapher's hand straightened. He carefully slipped a little piece of folded paper into the former sheriff's palm in this manner. Then he withdrew his hand, never once altering his expression, bobbed his head curtly at the sheriff, and walked on back the way he'd come.

His fist closed, MacCallister mounted up and watched as his son-in-law did the same, then the

65

pair of them rode on out into the brightly lighted roadway and headed northward out of town.

They were two miles along toward the country around Cheyenne Pass before MacCallister looped his reins, tilted his hat, and carefully unfolded the little slip of pale yellow paper in his hand. He read the thing, pursed up his lips, and read it again.

Klinger asked: "What's it say?"

The sheriff obviously thought this second copy of a telegram was the answer to the wire his father-in-law had sent south the day before. But it wasn't at all. The paper that the telegrapher had slipped Ethan was a duplicate of the telegram Ray Thorne had sent to Denver the previous day.

"It says," MacCallister told him, "that Thorne has hired four local men. That you and I are obstructing justice up here in Winchester. That we're on the side of DeFore, and that Thorne needs reinforcements or at least funds to hire reinforcements."

Klinger sat astride his horse, looking dumbfounded. "Let me see that," he said.

Once MacCallister had passed the paper over, he reached into a pocket and drew forth the reply to his own telegram, re-read this one, too, then handed it across. His reply, from the same source—the stage company's head office in Denver—said simply that an executive of the establishment was coming north to Winchester on the first stage.

The sheriff read and re-read both telegrams, before handing them back to MacCallister, saying: "That lousy gunfighter. I told you what he was trying to do, Ethan. He's stirring this up into a big brawl so's he can keep on drawing his professional gunfighter's salary."

MacCallister had no comment to make, not just because what John had said was the truth, but because, ahead of them about a mile, he caught the quick, sharp reflection of sunlight flashing off metal.

They were three miles out of Winchester now with the sun almost directly overhead. They were on DeFore's range and had been ever since leaving the stage road to swing inland, or easterly a little ways, so as to eventually strike the main road leading to DeFore's home ranch.

Klinger had a few more uncomplimentary things to say about Ray Thorne, but eventually, when he noticed his father-in-law's watchful silence, John stopped grousing, lifted his head with new awareness, and also began watching the roundabout country.

They were within sight of a commonly used, broad road which wound around the low-down slopes of rolling hills, when three cowboys suddenly appeared around a little knoll, stopped in the middle of the lawmen's pathway, blocking additional progress. They sat there, silent and watchful, until MacCallister and his son-in-law rode up. The leader of these men was bitter-eyed Travis Browne, who put his stoic stare upon Klinger with obvious hostility, saying nothing.

"Mister DeFore around?" MacCallister asked, pretending not to notice the quick resentment between the two former friends.

Browne continued to stare at Klinger before he finally swung his attention to MacCallister. He nodded. "Yeah, he's around, Ethan. But he isn't seeing anyone today."

"No? I don't see it that way. I reckon he'll see us, Travis."

"No, he won't. Before we rode out, he said he didn't want to see you . . . or him"—he shot a hostile look at his former rival—"particularly."

"Well now," Ethan said gently, "I'd like to make this a friendly call, Travis, but if that can't be done, why then I'll make it official."

"Ethan, you're trespassing."

John Klinger opened his mouth to speak. His face was darkening the longer this exchange went on.

MacCallister made a little silencing gesture and half smiled at Browne. "You don't know much law, do you?" he said. "So, Travis, before you do something we will all be sorry about, let me explain something to you. The law of this territory specifically states that a man's front door must be available to all public officials."

"I don't give a . . ."

"Easy, Travis, easy. You've walked a pretty narrow trail ever since this fight began. Don't step off on the wrong side now."

"I got my orders," the foreman insisted.

"All right, but to law enforcement officials they don't apply, and if you push for trouble, you're going to be an outlaw ten minutes from now."

MacCallister and Browne stared hard at one another. MacCallister was no longer looking friendly; he wasn't even looking amiable anymore. This was a stand-off. Someone had to back down and MacCallister was forcing Browne into a showdown.

He asked: "Where is DeFore . . . at the house?"

Browne nodded.

"Then suppose you take us to him . . . like maybe you took us prisoner or something. That might just let you off the hook. At least it'll show DeFore you were on the job." MacCallister lifted his rein hand, kneed out his horse, and started past. As he came up even with Browne, he said quietly: "One other thing. The next time you lads lie atop a hill keeping watch . . . you might consider wrapping cloth around your carbine barrels. We picked up the reflection a mile off."

Klinger smirked as he rode past.

For several moments Browne bitterly watched

the two before he moved. Then he jerked his head at the riders with him, looking dour, and the trio of cowboys followed along, walking their horses down to the main road leading to the DeFore Ranch.

Nothing was said until the ranch buildings were in sight—massive log structures aged and weathered, but like their owner, solid as granite and knowledgeably seasoned.

Browne, making a particular point of ignoring Klinger, said: "We heard that fancy-Dan of a gunfighter is Ray Thorne. Is that true, Ethan?"

"Plumb right."

"Then we should've killed him day before yesterday at the pass," the range boss hissed.

"Or gotten killed yourself," muttered the sheriff.

Browne swung his head to look the sheriff in the eye. "Six to one?" he reminded him.

"Yeah, six to one, Browne," Klinger stated. "He had six slugs in each gun, and from the stories I've heard about Thorne, he could've emptied your saddles in five seconds."

"Maybe," Browne grumbled, looking ahead where a big raw-boned, older man, having sighted the cavalcade of horsemen in his roadway, came walking out into the ranch yard to squint outward, seeking to identify them. "Maybe we'll get another chance to see about that."

MacCallister was silent as he considered the

big, craggy, roughly dressed and tough-standing older man on ahead. He'd known Richard DeFore a long time. They'd never been especially good friends—they were too entirely different for that—but they'd both shown respect for the other at different times over the years and Ethan could see, while he was still a hundred yards off, that DeFore finally had recognized him.

When the five riders drew to a halt within twenty feet of DeFore, close enough to see his hard-set jaw and his uncompromising steely eyes, Browne spoke up.

"Ran into 'em on their way here. Brought 'em in because they pulled the law on me."

Richard DeFore was at least fifteen years older than Ethan MacCallister. From the looks of him he had to be at least sixty, maybe sixty-five. But there wasn't an ounce of surplus flesh on him anywhere. He was flat and angular with snow-white hair that curled out from under a well-worn and tugged-forward old black Stetson hat. His mouth was a long, bloodless slit above a powerful jaw and his eyes were as direct, as challenging and fearless, as a man's eyes could be. He exuded hostility now, and, as John Klinger had once observed, he was a prickly man full of yeasty pride and abruptness.

Without wasting time on greetings, he looked from MacCallister to Klinger and said sharply: "What do you want here?"

"Talk," MacCallister answered for his son-in-law, "without an audience."

DeFore balanced this in his mind, jerked his head at Browne and the other two riders, waited until those men had reined off toward a log bunkhouse across the yard, then said commandingly: "Talk!"

MacCallister didn't dismount. He hadn't been asked to, which was an almost unforgivable breach of cow-country etiquette. He could see, from the corner of his eye, that John was getting mad at this insolent treatment, so he spoke quickly, in this way hoping to divert his son-in-law's hostility.

"We'd take it as a favor if you'd keep your riders out of town for a few days," MacCallister said.

"Why?" barked the grizzled old cowman. "You afraid they'll cut down that fancy-Dan of a gunfighter, Ethan?"

"The other way around. I don't want Thorne cutting them down."

"Hah! One lousy gunfighter! Even this Ray Thorne isn't going to cut down any DeFore riders. I don't hire weaklings and you know it."

"Won't be just Thorne facing your cowboys," stated MacCallister, and although he added nothing to this, the implication was amply clear.

He and Richard DeFore steadily regarded one another.

"You?" asked the old cowman.

"Us," corrected MacCallister.

"Taking the stage company's side?" DeFore said, sneering.

"You know a damned sight better than that. We're supposed to keep the peace, and that includes keeping three or six, or even a hundred, DeFore riders from jumping one gunfighter."

DeFore swung his bleak look on over to Klinger. He silently but scornfully considered the sheriff's badge on John's shirt front. His look spoke volumes but he didn't say a word.

"Couple of days isn't much," MacCallister stated, bringing the older man's attention back to himself. "There's an official of the stage line coming up from Denver. If you'll keep your men . . . specially Travis Browne . . . out of town until after he arrives, I'll bring him up here and you two can maybe work out your differences. If you don't . . . if you turn Travis and the others loose on Thorne . . . you'll blow this whole thing sky-high."

"Why shouldn't it be blown sky-high . . . tell me that."

"You know the answer to that as well as I do. John and I don't care how this thing is settled. All we want is to be sure that it *is* settled. And by legal means, not by your guns or Thorne's guns." MacCallister leaned across his saddle horn and stared at DeFore before saying: "You don't really want a shooting war any more than we do, Dick."

"Oh, I don't, don't I?"

"No, you don't . . . because the minute you break the law you know cussed well you're going to lose."

Again DeFore ran his bleak, hostile look over to John Klinger, but this time he addressed the sheriff. "Boy, you used to be a pretty fair range rider. Whatever made you think you'd be a good sheriff, too?"

Klinger stepped down off his horse, took five big steps forward, and halted with less than three feet separating him from big Richard DeFore. His eyes flashed fire points and his lips were sucked flat against his teeth.

"Because I couldn't see myself spending the rest of my life working for damned old despots like you, and because a man never knows what he's good at until he tries."

DeFore's steely gaze never wavered but his nostrils flared at this fiery confrontation. He was not used to being faced down and he would not permit this to happen. Speaking very softly, the rancher said: "Get back on that horse, Sheriff, and don't you ever challenge me again as long as you live. You hear?" He paused, shifted his gaze to run it down Klinger and back up again. In the same quiet but lethal tone he then added: "Let me tell you something, boy. That badge doesn't

74

mean a thing until you learn that more than a fast draw's got to go with it."

"What do you mean by that?" demanded Klinger, ready to fight, almost eager to fight.

DeFore turned and started walking stiffly, his legs obviously bothering him, on across the ranch yard toward the bunkhouse.

Ethan kept watching the cowman until DeFore was out of earshot, then, still keeping his gaze riveted on DeFore, he said sharply to his son-in-law: "Do like he said. Get back on that damned horse."

Klinger turned to shoot his father-in-law a smoky, bitter glare. As he did this, Richard DeFore halted, swung, and called over to the older lawman.

"Two days, MacCallister," he called. "Two days and no more."

DeFore swung back and continued stamping on over to the bunkhouse.

MacCallister let his body turn loose in the saddle. He finally dropped his eyes. "Get in the saddle, John, and let's get on back to town."

They were a mile southward back down through the hills before either of them spoke again. It was midafternoon and it was hot.

MacCallister was the first to speak. "Son, I hope you learned a lesson back there. You can't fight a man like Richard DeFore without having a war. But you can give him enough cold facts to show him the futility of fighting you."

Glumly, John responded: "Another tomfool play. Ethan, I think I ought to resign as sheriff."

First, the shotgun guard had quit. Then Hank Weaver had threatened to quit. Now John was saying the same thing. MacCallister was getting weary of hearing those words.

CHAPTER SEVEN

The day was beginning to turn cool and misty by the time they arrived back at the livery barn, put up their animals, and soberly hiked on down to the jailhouse. As soon as they were inside, both of them headed for the water bucket. Klinger drank first. Being second, MacCallister took his time taking his fill.

When Ethan set down the dipper to run his shirt sleeve across his mouth, John announced: "I'll resign and you can have the job back." Then he walked over to a chair near the door and dropped wearily down upon it.

Ethan finished drinking, hung the dipper on the designated nail above the bucket. He turned to gaze upon his son-in-law. "I don't think I want the job again," he told him. "So, if you quit and I don't take the job, who's left to take over?"

John looked baffled. "What are you getting at?"

"Well, if neither of us want to be sheriff, then it'd be up to the town council to appoint a successor, and let me tell you, John, with someone like Ray Thorne in town, no one would be willing to take it. So Sherman County would most likely be left without any law right at the time it needed it more than it has in the last ten years."

The former sheriff crossed to the desk, tossed his hat down, and rummaged around in his pockets for his makings. When he found the sack and papers, he went to work building a smoke.

"Tell you something else," he said, frowning with concentration as he made a trough for the tobacco. "If you were out of the game and I was out of it, it wouldn't surprise me none at all if Thorne himself would try for the job."

"You're kidding," John said, aghast at this possibility.

"No, I'm not kidding. He wouldn't be the first gunfighter who got a badge and wore it, and he certainly won't be the last." Ethan lighted the cigarette. "And don't underestimate Thorne, either. He'd know in a minute how valuable that badge would be to him. Not just against DeFore, but against anyone else who got in his way. Within months Winchester would become a safe haven for more outlaws, gamblers, gunfighters in it than . . ."

"The town council would never appoint a man like Thorne," Klinger broke in, standing up and dismissing what his father-in-law was saying with a wave his hand.

"No? If no one else volunteered they'd have to, John. You can't run a place as big and as raw as Sherman County without any law. They'd not only have to appoint Thorne, but he'd make damned sure no one else volunteered for the job."

MacCallister paused to smoke, watching his son-in-law through the gathering bluish haze. When he could see that John's indignation over Ray Thorne possibly succeeding him as sheriff was crystallizing into solid opposition, he said: "Listen, you keep on learning about men like you did today out at DeFore's place, and I still say you'll make the best danged peace officer Sherman County's ever had."

Before John could reply to that—if he intended to—the road-side door opened and Clem Whipple stepped into their office.

Without any preliminaries, Clem said: "Boys, them two mean-lookin' customers you ordered out of town this mornin', didn't go. They're over at the Teton Saloon right now with Thorne and two others who look just about like 'em."

MacCallister sighed, ran a resigned look over at Klinger, and shook his head. "One thing after another," he said. "Clem, were you in the Teton?"

"Yeah. The five of 'em were sittin' at a poker table with a bottle, talkin' back and forth. Ethan, it looked almighty suspicious to me."

"Clem, how'd you like to be deputized?" asked MacCallister.

The wiry little stage driver's eyes turned wide with apprehension. "Not me," he said in quick protest. "I'm not the gun-slingin' kind. No, sir." Then he ducked his head in a hasty nod at the two lawmen, whirled around, and passed swiftly

79

back out of the office, closing the door carefully as if he were sneaking out.

Klinger smiled. "Odd thing about people," he observed. "They want law and order but they don't want to take any risks to achieve it."

"You're learning, son, you're learning," MacCallister said as he picked up his hat, sat it low on the back of his head, and headed over to the door. "Well, come on, we told them to leave town and they didn't, so now we pick 'em up, fetch 'em back here, and arrange for their keep."

They walked out into the cooling afternoon, crossed the road, and struck along northward toward the Teton Saloon. In front of the stage office, Clem had joined Weaver upon the passenger bench bolted to the wall. Both were sitting there dejectedly.

Upon seeing the two there, MacCallister said to John out of the corner of his mouth: "See Hank and Clem over there? You can learn something from them, too. Everyone likes to witness a fight, and, badge or no badge, how you handle yourself determines whether folks sympathize with you or turn against you."

They came to the saloon's bat-wing doors, shoved on through, looked around casually at first before crossing over to the bar. Behind them at a table near the door was the gunfighter. He was as aware of the two lawmen as they were of him. MacCallister noted immediately that Thorne had only two men sitting there with him, not four, and the two rough-looking riders who had been ordered out of town were not the two at the table.

He leaned against the bar counter and sighed audibly as Rusty Millam came strolling up. "Two ales," he said to Millam as he twisted and made a wry face at John. "That's how it goes sometimes. You walk into a place expecting something . . . and grab a hand full of empty air."

Hearing this, Millam looked at MacCallister as he set the glasses down. He checked out Thorne's table and, leaning in, he said barely above a whisper: "If you were expecting Thorne to have more than two fellows with him, you got here about ten minutes too late."

MacCallister took a healthy chug of his ale. It was tangy and it was cold. "There were others?" he confirmed.

Rusty nodded. "Yeah, the two men you ordered out of town. They were here for an hour. Thorne and them others sat around over there, drinking and mumbling, then those two from before walked out. I saw 'em get their horses from the livery barn and head out of town."

"Which way?" Klinger asked.

Millam shrugged. "Got busy right then and didn't notice. I'll bet Lemuel can tell you over at the livery barn though."

MacCallister said: "Good idea, Rusty. Thanks."

He finished his ale, dropped a coin on the bar top, and turned to John, saying: "Drink up."

Klinger made no prompt move to depart even though his glass was empty. Instead, he ran a slow look around the saloon and ran head-on into the steady, cold gaze of Ray Thorne. Those two stared until the sheriff deliberately turned his back, leaned upon the bar top, commenting to MacCallister: "Let's take all three of 'em in."

"Can't. Got no grounds that would hold up. This is what you got to be real careful about . . . never let folks start accusing you of persecuting them or anyone else."

Klinger snorted and then grimaced, wishing there was something he could do to Thorne and the group he was putting together.

MacCallister smiled at him, brushed his son-in-law's arm to indicate they should leave. They covered the ground to the door slowly, passed the poker table where the frozen-faced men watched their every move, and then were out upon the roadway again.

As they struck out for the livery barn, Klinger voiced the opinion that while he was beginning to understand some things which heretofore he'd never thought much about regarding law enforcement work, he wasn't convinced those things were right.

"That," the former sheriff declared emphatically, "is the first sign that you're becoming a lawman.

You're never supposed to take sides in disputes
. . . that's the lawman's code . . . and yet you're
human, so you have sympathies whether you're
supposed to or not. The trick is . . . and it's hard
. . . not to show anything. I wish it was easy. Like
now . . . Thorne's actions would rub any lawman
the wrong way. But on the other hand, old Dick
DeFore isn't exactly winning any popularity
contest with me, either. So it's thinking about
these things that makes it easy . . . for me at least
. . . to remain neutral. But I don't think things
will stay like this. They never do where anger and
high-strung feelings are concerned. Still, you've
got to remain strictly neutral . . . no matter what."

When MacCallister glanced over at his son-
in-law, he could see he was listening closely
to everything he was saying. While he was
looking a little perplexed, he also seemed much
less resentful than MacCallister had expected.
The former sheriff looked ahead, taking in the
doorless maw of the livery barn, and he smiled
inwardly. He was encouraged that John seemed
to be learning. Ethan was determined to make a
first-class law officer of him yet. Still, he didn't
like the idea of a mess like this simmering feud
between DeFore and the stage company being
John's first taste of law enforcement work.

Just before the pair stepped up onto the plank
walk by the livery barn though, MacCallister told
himself that perhaps getting embroiled in a big

lot of trouble right at the outset wasn't so bad, either, since John would likely learn the basic things he had to know all at once instead of, as Ethan had wished, over a period of years.

Time would tell, he told himself. Time would prove whether John had what it took to be a worthwhile sheriff of Sherman County or not, and while time was working that out, Ethan MacCallister would concentrate upon keeping his son-in-law from getting killed, for the sake of his daughter.

Lemuel, the livery man, was rigging out a top buggy for a pair of middle-aged women. He saw MacCallister, nodded, and signaled that he'd be along as soon as he was finished, then hurried to get the buggy ready.

The two lawmen went over by the office door set up in the corner of the barn and waited there. It was dingy in this place, and it smelled strongly of hay and ammonia.

Klinger leaned back against the wall and drifted his moody gaze back out into the roadway where dusky shadows were drawing down. "Why don't you drop over for supper tonight?" he said to his father-in-law.

"I'll do that. One thing about being single . . . a man sure gets tired of eating in local beaneries."

Waving the wagon out once the women were settled on it, Lemuel ambled over, mopping his several pendulous chins with a greasy red bandanna. He planted himself squarely in front of the lawmen and raised his eyebrows.

"We've been told that two hard-bitten cowboys rode out of here an hour or so back," MacCallister said. "Hoping you saw them and know which way they headed out."

"Them the two you and John told to get out of town this mornin'?"

"The same two."

Lemuel scratched his nodding head. "They rode north, but it weren't no hour ago. I'd say it was more like two hours."

Something suddenly seemed to hit Klinger hard. He drew himself upright and grabbed the livery man by the shoulders, looking like he wanted to shake him before he let go. Then he calmed himself down and asked: "Think back . . . this is important . . . did you hear those two say anything?"

Lemuel pulled out his bandanna again, beginning to sweat at Klinger's urgency. "Did they say anythin'?" Lemuel echoed. "Well, I wasn't payin' too much attention. You know how it is . . . drifters come and drifters go." He raised his beefy shoulders in a shrug. "They talked a little but I can't rightly recollect any of what it was about."

MacCallister was puzzled by John's impatience, so he put a hand on John's shoulder and said: "What is it? What's in your craw?"

85

But the sheriff didn't answer. Instead, he thanked Lemuel, and, taking Ethan's arm, walked back out upon the yonder plank walk. There, he stopped, let go of Ethan's arm, and said: "I've been telling you all day Thorne would figure out ways of keeping this thing going. We stopped his stage this morning. We also went out to DeFore's and got his pledge to keep the peace."

"All right," MacCallister said. "What of it?"

"Ethan, those two didn't leave town like they were told to. They sat around in plain sight all day, until we got back. That's gotta mean that Thorne's having us watched. Think about it. The minute we return to town, Thorne sends those two away."

"Go on."

"Northward, Ethan. That's up toward Cheyenne Pass. I don't know what he's up to, but I'm telling you again that Thorne's setting up some kind of bad trouble."

MacCallister studied his son-in-law's features in the gloomy dusk for a thoughtful moment, thinking over what he had just said. He threw a long look over toward the Teton Saloon and then it struck him as powerfully now as it had earlier struck John. Thorne had not given up at all when twice he'd been circumvented in his efforts to start a fight. Instead, he had struck out on a new, more devious course, to achieve the same ends.

"You know," he said as he continued to stare at the Teton, "I'm beginning to think you've got something here, John. To the north isn't only Cheyenne Pass, but DeFore's ranch."

"We'd better do some riding," Klinger said, turning toward the livery barn. "But we'd better do it separately. One of us should scout the pass to be sure Thorne's men aren't setting up some kind of a bushwhack up there. The other ought to head over to DeFore's ranch and have a good look around. I wouldn't put it past Thorne to pay to have someone killed . . . maybe Travis Browne, or maybe even DeFore himself."

Ethan turned as John started forward. For a moment he simply watched his son-in-law moving toward the barn with a newfound determination. Then he followed John back into the barn.

It made him feel good inside, the way John had finally grasped the entire idea of what they were up against. He wasn't thoroughly satisfied that those two hirelings of Thorne's hadn't heard that the sheriff and his deputy were returning to town, and had therefore decided it would be prudent to leave as they'd been ordered to do. But even if it meant riding around all night in the northward hills, Ethan was willing to do it, just to encourage John to think as a lawman.

Lemuel retrieved their animals, stood by as each lawman rigged out his own beast, and as they rose up over leather, he wished them: "Good huntin', boys."

John looked down from atop his horse. "Lemuel, you could do me a favor if you wanted to."

"Shoot," said the livery man. "Anythin' you want, Sheriff."

"Go by my house and tell Ruth I might not be home for supper."

Lemuel nodded with understanding. "Consider it done. After thirty years of married life I know exactly how to handle women on things like that."

MacCallister smiled to himself. Lemuel's wife was a holy terror. He put up a bold front away from the house, but never within earshot of his wife.

CHAPTER EIGHT

There was no moon when full night finally came down across the land. All the little winking stars didn't shed much light, either, because the heavens were a soot-like black. But it was a warm night, and barring the lack of light, it was pleasant enough as MacCallister and his son-in-law rode on through town and out upon the northward stage road.

They spoke a little, desultorily, as they rode along, mostly reviewing what had thus far occurred in their struggle to keep the DeFore faction from meeting the stage-line gunfighter.

Klinger said: "We're still ahead, Ethan. That stage company fellow ought to arrive tomorrow. All we'll have to do then is get him to sit down with DeFore."

The sheriff smiled broadly when MacCallister shot him a skeptical look before saying: "Yeah, nothing to it. About like getting General Custer and Sitting Bull to sit down and have a nice talk."

They laughed, then rode in silence until they came to the initial lift in the land leading on up into Cheyenne Pass. There they paused to look and listen and make some decisions.

"I'll go on up into the pass," Klinger said. "You head for the DeFore place."

He had barely gotten the words out when a sudden rush of unseen horses on ahead up the trail brought both lawmen straight up in their saddles. The running horses made their passing quickly, and within moments all sound of their hoofs had disappeared into the night.

The younger man looked all around, plainly puzzled.

"More than just two riders," he said.

The older man didn't comment for a long while, but when he did, it was clear that he was no longer in favor of splitting up.

"Passing from east to west on across the road. That's when we heard 'em . . . when they hit the roadway. After that they hit tall grass. John, we better forget about DeFore's ranch. I think whatever's going on, lies directly ahead. Come on . . . but we need to be careful and as quiet as we can be."

They didn't hasten for the same reason they'd been able to hear those other riders. Cheyenne Pass was rock hard from decades of travel, and in some places it was rocky enough to carry the clatter of shod hoofs for a long distance.

They were nearing the final long incline leading up to the place where, several days earlier, they had turned back the stage and met Ray Thorne for the first time. Ethan lifted his hand and, because it was so dark, said John's name as softly as he could to bring him to halt.

Around them where they sat, the night was scented with roiled dust and a lingering smell of horse sweat, but there wasn't a sound of those riders to be detected.

MacCallister tried to sight movement against the skyline, failed. They moved off the road in a westerly direction. They went along, still making no imprudent haste despite the muffling grass underfoot, until, far off, one solitary gunshot reverberated, shattering all the otherwise stillness of this troubled night. Then Ethan booted his animal over into a slow lope and went down the land toward the explosion.

There was no answering shot, so, when they came to an open side-hill where they could ride abreast, John said: "They either got him or lost him."

"Got him," stated MacCallister. "Otherwise, he'd have fired back." He reined suddenly to a quick halt and said: "Listen."

The sound of riders came again, but quieter this time, and slower. Those invisible mounted men were evidently fanning out and beating the underbrush as they rode northward through this up-ended country. Neither of the lawmen sighted any of those men, but after a moment of listening, MacCallister said: "Not as many now as there were when they crossed the road."

"It's got to be DeFore's riders," murmured

John. "No other outfit is up in the Cheyenne Pass country."

"Sure, it'll be DeFore's riders, but what's interesting me right about now is who fired that shot and why."

"Maybe they ran across Thorne's two men. They sure as hell were after someone when they crossed the road."

MacCallister kept his head cocked until he'd placed the position of those unseen riders, then he eased out again, motioning with his free hand for John to be very quiet, even though he knew it was too dark for his partner to see the movement.

They had traveled nearly another full mile westward before they both saw the little flickering brightness of a struck match down in a gloomy, narrow cañon. Ethan grunted with satisfaction, dismounted, tied his horse, and, carbine in hand, started stealthily forward. Behind him, John also tugged free his Winchester and came along.

The cañon was a narrow, dark place, made darker by this inky night sky, with a tangle of oaks growing in its marshy bottom. Both sides, despite their abruptness, were grassy and not too sloping for easy access.

MacCallister, scouting ahead of Klinger a hundred feet or so, started down. He paused once to let John come up.

"Stay behind me and try to follow where I step. If we keep to the tall grass, we won't scuff loose stones and let whoever's down there know we're coming."

John agreed to try his best to follow in his father-in-law's footsteps. A half hour later the pair of them got all the way down where a little sluggish trickle of creek water aimlessly meandered, making the cañon's narrow floor verdant and at the same time soggy.

Another match flared, halting both the lawmen. MacCallister had the location of that third man in this gloomy place fixed in his mind and needed no additional guidance, so he halted to wait for the light to flicker out. When it did, he started onward again.

It was relatively simple to move slowly along now without making a sound. The difficulty was in seeing. It had been hard enough in this poorly lighted night to make things out up above, but down in this cañon it was much darker, much wilder with all the profuse, tangled growth, and because of this MacCallister struck his left foot against something which yielded to the touch but did not move, and he fell, whispering an angry curse as he flung out a hand to break the fall.

That hand came in contact with something furry and warm. He drew it quickly back, rolled to his knees, and strained to see into the surrounding darkness. It was impossible to make out shapes or silhouettes so he put his hand gingerly forward again, found that same yielding warm and furry object, groped along it, felt something harder but also yielding, and leaned far forward to identify whatever it was that had tripped him.

He reared back, turned to put his head close to John's ear, and whispered: "Dead horse with a saddle on it. I reckon that shot didn't hit a man after all. It hit a horse."

Somewhere ahead a man's soft groan faintly echoed. MacCallister whipped back around, placed that sound, and eased gingerly around the dead horse. He took one long step at a time, paused between strides to listen, and came to a parting in the gloomy trees where faint starshine shone eerily upon a clearing of gravelly soil unfit to support vegetation. There, flat out and discernible, was the shape of a man.

Ethan brought up his carbine, trained it forward, took in a deep breath, and stepped out into that small clearing.

The downed man heard something and could make out vaguely what he thought to be the silhouette of a man. He stared into the black, wrinkling his brow in a mighty effort to identify the shape, couldn't, and let his head drop back.

"Shoot and be damned to you," the man muttered thickly.

MacCallister went closer, leaned his Winchester upon a rock, and knelt beside the man. Klinger stood off a little, watching the shadows of this ghostly place without relinquishing his carbine.

He was not as interested in the identity of the injured man near his feet as he evidently was in the possibility of there being enemies in the surrounding night.

MacCallister bent far over, looked, straightened back, and said: "It's Travis Browne and he's been bad hurt."

Klinger seemed to relax at the announcement. He shuffled in a little closer, grounded his carbine, and bent earthward, trying to make out DeFore's ranch foreman. He couldn't really see him, so he asked: "Can you tell if he was shot or just hurt from the fall after his horse was shot?"

MacCallister got Browne's head up and his shoulders cradled in his arm. He gently shook the injured man. "Travis? Travis, what happened? Who fired that shot and what was all the rough riding about?"

Browne stirred a little, tried to make out the face of the man who was asking him questions.

"It's me . . . MacCallister. What happened, Travis?"

"Ethan?" Browne said, his hand moving up to his head. "How'd you get here? Were you one of them?"

"One of who, Travis?"

Browne closed his eyes and groaned.

Klinger bent to catch what the injured man was saying.

"It was two . . . ," Browne began weakly, and

then his words trailed off. Suddenly his eyes opened as though he had been startled. "You two, by gawd. Ethan . . . you and John . . . Sold out . . . didn't you? I'll be . . . damned. . . ."

Then Browne's head rolled slightly to the right, his body went limp, and MacCallister eased him back down upon the ground. The deputy sheriff ran his hands along Browne's body in an attempt to determine how he had been injured.

"Dead . . . is he dead?" John asked, sounding a trifle breathless.

"Passed out," MacCallister responded. "We've got to get him up out of here and into town where a doctor can look him over. I can't feel any blood, so I'm thinking the shot must've killed his horse and then the two of 'em rolled down into this cañon." Ethan stood up and craned his neck to look up the ghostly side-hill, but it was pointless.

He let out a sigh, then let out a string of curses before saying to John: "Why the devil didn't he break his own fall? Why did he have to tumble this far down? He's no flyweight. We're going to have the devil's own time getting him up out of here."

Klinger didn't seem too disturbed by the news, but that was only because he was troubled about something else.

"What did he mean when he said we sold out? Do you think he knew what he was saying?"

MacCallister rocked back on his heels and

gazed thoughtfully down at the unconscious Browne. "No, I don't think he was. Seems he thinks we've taken the stage-line's side."

Ethan craned for another look up the side-hill, then said: "John, you were plumb right. Thorne sent his two hardcases up here for some no-good purpose. I reckon old man DeFore expected someone might try something up here so he had his crew on watch. Travis here, and his friends, jumped the hardcases, chased them, evidently lost 'em in the night and were beating the underbrush for 'em when we heard the riders going north."

"And one of them got off a lucky shot," Klinger observed, rounding out MacCallister's deductions, "and knocked down Travis's horse."

"Yeah, what luck is it that deposits a man as heavy as Travis Browne down in this danged place, then puts us here to pack him out again?" MacCallister bent over. "Well, come on, John, let's get started with it."

They picked up DeFore's range boss and began edging their way uphill. It was hard work. Even if Browne hadn't been dish-rag limp, he still would have been a solid burden. He was a thick-shouldered, oaken-legged man as heavy as lead. They had to stop often on the way up. By the time they eventually reached the place where they'd left their animals, MacCallister dropped down in the grass and remained motionless and breathing heavily for a full fifteen minutes. He appeared

97

no longer interested in Travis Browne at all.

When Klinger straightened up from a close examination of Browne and called out his father-in-law's name, Ethan raised up to look and listen.

"He's got some cracked ribs and I think his left arm is broken," John informed him.

"Too bad it wasn't his right arm," Ethan growled, pushing himself upright off the flinty earth. "That way his gun hand would be out of commission. I've got a feeling that from tonight on we might wish all of DeFore's men had busted their gun arms."

John pondered what his father-in-law had said as he got up and started toward their horses. Suddenly he halted, turned, and looked back. "DeFore?" he said softly. "You thinking what I think you're thinking, Ethan?"

"Yeah. Thorne sent those riders of his up here where they got no business being to do something they probably had no business doing. They got caught . . . at least they got chased . . . and one of 'em downed DeFore's foreman on DeFore's land. And if that doesn't add up to a shooting war, I don't know what does."

MacCallister sighed and stepped over to consider Browne's gray and slack face. He shook his head at the unconscious man. "I'll tell you something else too, John," he growled. "Ray Thorne didn't really care whether those two men of his got chased or not. He didn't even care whether they got caught or not. All he wanted was to force someone to fire a shot. Well, someone did. Thorne's scheme worked. Here lies Dick DeFore's foreman who old Dick admires and treats like a son, and Thorne's finally succeeded in forcing a fight." He paused to shake his head, then said: "Here, give me a hand putting Travis on my horse. Then we'd best get back to town."

They strained to settle Browne across the saddle and, after pausing briefly to catch their breath, lashed him there. They began their painfully slow descent back toward town, taking turns riding Ethan's horse to keep Browne steady and in the saddle.

It was close to midnight before they arrived back in Winchester, and Browne had stirred only twice, very briefly. Each time he had recognized his companions and cursed them. The last time MacCallister had curtly explained how the two of them had happened to be up in Cheyenne Pass, but before he even had this recital half told, Browne passed out again.

They routed the local doctor, carried Browne into the doctor's treatment room in the lower part of his home, put him on a table, and sank down wearily to await the outcome of the medical man's examination.

Klinger's prognosis turned out to be correct up to a point. Browne had a broken left arm and three cracked ribs. He also had a concussion, and this, the doctor explained, was why Browne kept passing out on the way back to town.

"Fix him up," ordered the former sheriff. "Do whatever has to be done, Doc."

Then the lawmen left, halted upon the empty plank walk outside, and looked at one another solemnly.

"All right," MacCallister declared. "We go after Thorne now."

CHAPTER NINE

MacCallister and Klinger went across to the hotel and up to Ray Thorne's room, but the gunfighter was not there. They returned to the outer hallway where Klinger said: "At this time of night he's not at the saloons because they were shutting down when we came in around midnight. So where would he be?"

MacCallister shrugged. He was tired and he ached all over from their recent exertions. He was also disgruntled at not finding Thorne, but all he said was: "Go on home, John. We'll hunt him down in the morning."

They parted outside the hotel, John homeward bound, Ethan heading for Winchester's only all-night café. After he filled up on coffee and food, he returned to the hotel, went directly to his room, and retired. He was drowsy enough, he thought, to sleep for a week, but by five in the morning he was wide awake, so he got up, shaved, went down to the dining room, and had a big breakfast.

It bothered him that Ray Thorne had been out all night. There were of course several perfectly logical reasons for the gunfighter's absence from his room, but MacCallister wasn't so sure any of them applied.

He went over to the jailhouse, stoked up the stove, placed the coffee pot on it, and sat down to have his after-breakfast smoke before his son-in-law showed up. He was sitting there putting together little pieces of thoughts, trying to form something whole, when the doctor walked in.

MacCallister smiled but his eyes remained serious. "You're up early," he said to the medical man by way of greeting. Dr. Benjamin Shirley was a young man, very focused and often brusque. He was relatively new to Winchester.

"When someone dumps an injured man on my doorstep in the middle of the night I sometimes don't get to bed at all," he said, owlishly regarding the deputy sheriff.

"Well hell, Doc, we found him hurt up in Cheyenne Pass. What were we supposed to do?"

"Exactly what you did, of course, but that still doesn't improve my chances for sleep. Anyway, he's in much better shape this morning. He has the constitution of an ox."

"Glad to hear he's improving."

"He wants to see you, Deputy."

"I can imagine," he murmured. "Last night, on the ride back into town, all he did when he was conscious was cuss out the sheriff and me."

"I know. He was still doing it this morning until I told him it was you two who brought him in. Then he said he wanted to talk to you."

MacCallister nodded. He offered the doctor some coffee, but after glancing over at the black, unwashed pot on the stove, the medical man declined and departed.

Ten minutes later Klinger arrived looking still sleep puffy. It was a sort of ritual that son-in-law and father-in-law scarcely spoke to one another until they'd had their coffee, so Ethan said nothing of the doctor's visit until they'd each downed a full cup of java. Ethan then explained about Browne wanting to see them, so they headed out of the office and up the empty walkway to the doctor's house.

Browne was on a cot in the dispensary. He had been bandaged and looked in much worse shape from all the swaddling than he actually was. His ribs were not actually broken, and while his left arm was now in a sling and his head was bandaged, his concussion was not as serious as it might have been.

He stared at the two lawmen from a solemn face though, and offered neither of them a greeting. Instead, he said: "Thanks for bringing me in. Maybe I wasn't too clear in what I said last night. I don't rightly remember what I said."

The former sheriff propped his back against the wall and said: "Oh, you were clear enough. Couple of times you were pretty darned clear. Tell us what it was all about, Travis."

"Yeah," grunted the injured man, "after you tell

103

me what you two were doing riding around in the pass in the dark."

John said sharply: "We were looking for a couple of men who rode out of town an hour or two ahead of us."

Browne shifted his gaze from Ethan. He and Klinger looked steadily at one another for a long time, neither of them showing friendliness for the other. Then Browne said: "Who sent those men up into the pass?"

"That stage company gunfighter is our best guess, though we have no proof," answered the sheriff, still speaking crisply.

"I thought so," mumbled Browne, and he paused in thought before turning to MacCallister. "If you knew they were sent up there, why didn't you stop 'em?"

The deputy's temper was becoming a little ruffled at this sharpness from Browne. "We were at DeFore's ranch until late afternoon, if you'll think back, and it takes time to ride from there back to town. Those two hirelings of Thorne's left Winchester before we returned, so we couldn't very well prevent them from going up to the pass. Now listen, Travis, we want some answers. Were you up there with your ranch crew guarding the pass?"

"Yeah. Me and five others. Mister DeFore said he wouldn't put it past someone down here to try and get a coach through in the night."

"And when you first saw those two . . . what were they doing?"

"Riding up the road with their heads alert. I hailed 'em, they broke away westward, and we chased 'em. I was out front and we were gaining when the rearmost man turned and got off one shot. It killed my horse. The last thing I remember is rolling down that hill-side into the cañon where you two found me."

As he pushed himself away from the wall, MacCallister said with exasperation: "Why the devil didn't you give 'em enough rope so you could follow them and see what they were up to?"

Browne bristled at this. "My orders were to keep the road closed. That's what I was doing. If you want someone to play detective, you'd better import a real one."

Klinger stood by the door now, where he took one long last look at DeFore's segundo. He lifted the latch as he said: "Did you get a good enough look at those two so you'd recognize them again?"

Browne shook his head gingerly. "It was too dark and they broke away too fast. I can tell you one thing though. The fellow that had the slower horse had a bundle tied behind his cantle. When I first glimpsed it, I figured it was a bedroll and that the two of them were just drifters passing through the country. But as I got a little closer, when I was gaining on that one, I could see it was some kind of a sack tied fast to his rear skirts, too big for a bedroll, the wrong shape."

"Thanks, Travis. See you later," MacCallister said, nodding his head as he went on out of the room with his son-in-law.

When they were back in the roadway with the early-morning sunlight shining all around them, MacCallister halted, his brow wrinkling as he thought about what Browne had said.

"What would they be carrying?" he said to John.

The sheriff started to speak, but then looked northward up the roadway and grunted instead. Drawn around by his son-in-law's action, he turned his gaze in that direction.

Just entering town from the north plain were six riders. Prominently in the lead of those range men was old Richard DeFore mounted on a leggy bay horse.

MacCallister muttered an oath and swung a quick look over toward the Teton Saloon. He saw the swamper outside, emptying a bucket of dirty water into the street. He also observed that the hitch rack was empty and there was no other sign that Thorne or any of his hirelings might be inside.

He stepped off the plank walk and halted five feet out. Behind him the sheriff kept watching the slow-pacing gait of those six grim-faced horsemen. Up and down the opposing sideways, others were also watching those men, and rather quickly a silence descended over town. After all, the only time Richard DeFore came riding into Winchester like this was when he was stirred up, and it took no great powers of divination now to see that the old man's granite face was unsmiling.

Except for Dr. Shirley, the two lawmen, and maybe a few of the town snoops who always managed to find out the latest happenings, no one in Winchester yet knew what had occurred in the night. But obviously old man DeFore had something on his mind, so people began to speculate even before MacCallister halted the cavalcade by simply standing out in the roadway barring its forward progress.

DeFore didn't say a word. He twisted, untied a bundle from the back of his saddle, swung it forward, and let it fall a foot in front of MacCallister.

"Look inside," he said coldly, not addressing either of the two lawmen specifically.

MacCallister stooped, opened the sack's neck, and peered at the contents. He looked a long time. So long in fact that John headed over from the plank walk to see what the sack contained. He reached down and pulled out two taped bundles of dynamite sticks. There were four sticks in each bundle. Still in the sack was fifty feet of black fuse cord.

DeFore dismounted, looked over at the doctor's house. He turned toward Ethan and asked: "Is Travis in there?" Ethan nodded.

DeFore instructed his men: "Tie up. I want three of you to search the town till you find that damned gunfighter. You other two, wait here. Don't leave the horses." He then swung toward the lawmen again. "I'll see you two down at the jailhouse when I'm through in there." Then the big man led his horse over to the hitch rack where he dismounted and tied up his horse. As DeFore's riders began dismounting, the old man unceremoniously pushed on into the doctor's house.

While this was going on, the sheriff placed the dynamite back in the bag before picking it up. He glanced over at Shirley's house, made a quick nod at his father-in-law, and turned back toward the jailhouse.

Walking down the middle of the road, both were conscious of more curious faces appearing on the plank walks as word spread of the brief exchange that had occurred out in the roadway.

Once inside the jailhouse, Klinger emptied the sack upon a table and stood staring gravely, considering the conclusive evidence of what Ray Thorne had sent those two men up into the pass to accomplish.

"But why?" he asked Ethan. "What good would dynamiting the pass do?"

MacCallister was feeling more and more annoyed. Not entirely by what Thorne had plotted to do, but by Richard DeFore's war-like appearance in town, as well as the older man's contemptuous, lethal manner. He made a smoke, lighted it, and strolled over beside John to consider those taped-together dynamite sticks.

"It's fairly obvious," he said. "They didn't intend to block the road, John. Their purpose was to plant those charges about where they figured DeFore's men might be. I'd guess Thorne meant to take another coach, his two remaining hardcases, and make another run up into the pass. Only this time Browne and his crew wouldn't have stopped the coach. They'd have likely gotten themselves blown to smithereens. The two Thorne sent up there last night were probably supposed to hide in the rocks and await the coach. When Travis's crew started forward to halt the stage, those two would cut short fuses, lob the explosives, and even if they didn't kill all of DeFore's men, they'd sure put 'em out of action long enough for the coach to get through."

"But hell, Ethan . . . what's the purpose? I mean, suppose Thorne got through with a coach. What good would that do? There isn't another town for twenty-seven miles and . . ."

"Son, a man like Ray Thorne only figures one way. He doesn't care about the coach, the next town, or even the senselessness of breaking

DeFore's blockade. All he's concerned with right now is the simple fact that twice he's had the wind knocked out of his sails when he tried to break through. He doesn't care how he does it, or what happens afterward. All he wants to do is to prove to the world . . . as if the world cares . . . that no one can scare or stop two-gun Ray Thorne."

"For that he'd maybe kill six men with these home-made bombs?" John asked, taking up one of the dynamite clusters.

"For that," responded Ethan grimly, "he'd bomb this whole blessed town and everyone in it . . . not just DeFore's crew. John, we've got to find Thorne and we've got to find him fast."

The sheriff put down the dynamite and half turned at the sound of the road-side door opening.

Richard DeFore stepped into the room, looked over at the two lawmen with a great deal of bitterness before closing the door. He took two steps into the room and, without any trace of gratitude in his voice, said: "Thanks for bringing Travis in."

MacCallister barely inclined his head. He said nothing and neither did John. They waited, knowing DeFore would tell them what was on his mind without being asked, and he did just exactly that.

"Ethan, John, I want this gunfighter . . . this Ray Thorne. Where is he?"

The former sheriff shook his head at DeFore. "He's not in town. That's all I can tell you."

"Hell, I know that," snarled the grizzled old cowman. "I had my boys search all over for him. What I want to know is . . . where is he? Ethan, you got him in one of your back-room cells?"

"No."

DeFore stared skeptically at the deputy. "Mind if I check?" he said, a look of distrust still in his face.

MacCallister's face got rusty red. "You're damned right I mind if you look," he said. "I told you he wasn't here. Are you calling me a liar?"

DeFore stood a moment in silence. He saw the surge of fierce anger turn MacCallister stiff and fighting mad. He gently shook his head. "No. No, I'm not calling anyone a liar, Ethan. Not yet, anyway. But I'm going to tell you boys something. I want that man for what he did to Travis, and for what he had in mind with those dynamite sticks he sent those men up into the pass to use. I aim to get him, too, even if I have to comb every inch of the hills between here and my home place. When I do . . . I aim to hang him. Anyone with him will get hanged right along with him, unless they got awful good excuses."

MacCallister waited patiently until DeFore had said all he had to say. When the rancher had finished, he looked the older man squarely in the face, controlling the annoyance that was turning to anger and starting to boil in him. He made DeFore wait, just as the rancher had the two lawmen wait when he entered the jailhouse. Then he stated with emphasis: "Dick, we've known each other a lot of years. I never craved your company and I reckon you never craved mine, but, by golly, I always had a lot of respect for you that I sure don't have when you talk like that. You're not going to hang anybody. Not Thorne or any of his hirelings, and you'd better get that through your thick skull. Because if you try it, so help me, I'll see you buried up there in your lousy Cheyenne Pass sure as I'm a foot tall."

DeFore returned MacCallister's uncompromising glare. He backed to the door, shaking his head as he reached for the door latch. "There are different kinds of law, Ethan MacCallister, and I prefer the kind that was in this country when we were young men. You try and stop me from hanging that gunfighter and we'll see who goes into the ground with him . . . you or me."

DeFore went out the door, heaved it shut, leaving behind a rank and troubled atmosphere.

CHAPTER TEN

Neglected, MacCallister's cigarette had died so he relit it and his usually steady hands shook from suppressed anger. He flung down the match and avoided Klinger's gaze as he stepped over to the desk, perched upon the edge of it, and unconsciously swore.

"That's how quick things can change," he said ultimately. "Last night we thought we had everything under control. DeFore had agreed to stay out of town for two days and Thorne was on foot as far as taking a stage up into the pass was concerned. Now everything's changed and all hell's about to bust loose."

He glared at those two bundles of dynamite on the table in front of John. "Of all the lousy ways for men to fight . . . using things like that."

Considering the dynamite in silence for a moment, John said: "I wonder how much more of this stuff they have?"

MacCallister grunted. "Trot over to the general store. That's the only place Thorne could buy dynamite in Winchester. Find out if he bought it there, and, if so, how much he bought. At least maybe we can be sure of one thing in this mess."

Klinger departed on the errand. MacCallister killed his smoke, got himself a cup of coffee, and drank it. He was so full of resentment he didn't even notice the brew was cold, just sipped it steadily as he thought. He was pondering making a fresh pot of java when John returned.

"Eight sticks, Ethan," John informed him. "The same number that are here, so I guess we can quit worrying about that at least."

Ethan began to feel a little better as he shifted in the desk chair. It wasn't just this information which was responsible though. He had an idea forming in his mind. "Come on," he said, getting up, and striding over to the road-side door. "We've got a ride to make."

The pair of them hiked toward the livery barn, but on the way Ethan stopped in at the stage office, with John trailing some several feet behind him.

At sight of Weaver aimlessly studying some manifests, Ethan asked: "Hank, what time is that northbound stage due in town tomorrow morning?"

Weaver looked up, gazed a moment at the two lawmen who had entered so quietly he hadn't heard them, and answered: "Not until about noon. Why?"

Turning, MacCallister walked out without answering, John again following behind. The former sheriff strode briskly to the livery barn and called out to Lemuel for their horses. Not until the hostler came tumbling from the office to

114

obey that sharp order, did Ethan say a word to his son-in-law.

"I'm probably wrong," he confided. "But I sure hope I'm not. If you were Thorne, where would you be this morning?"

John puckered his brow and shrugged. "Hard to say. If I knew the DeFore crew was after me, I'd probably be as far away as I could get."

"But you wouldn't know that, John, because you'd have left town last night before you even knew whether or not those two hirelings got safely hidden up in the pass or not."

"Well, then I don't know."

"I'll tell you where you'd be. You'd be somewhere south of town along the stage road awaiting the appearance of that coach bringing in the company official from Denver. You'd be down there to get in your licks before the company man talked to anyone else. You'd have to do that, in order to justify what trouble you've caused to happen in town and on up in Cheyenne Pass."

The sheriff's eyes gradually widened until he snapped his fingers and said excitedly: "I'll be damned. Ethan, I think you're right." He hesitated a moment as the picture became clearer to him, then he added: "DeFore'll be combing the northward hills. He'll never find Thorne or Thorne's men."

"He might find two of 'em," contradicted

115

Ethan. "The last we heard, those two were heading north. Maybe they got around DeFore's riders and struck out back for town, but if they did, and they couldn't find Thorne, I doubt they'd stick around. Not after what happened up in the pass last night, and not after we ordered them out of the county."

"But it's possible those two knew Thorne was going to meet the northbound stage, and if they did, there's a good possibility they might have ridden on south to find him, wanting to tell him what happened up in the pass last night."

Ethan fell silent briefly, all the while thinking. It was then that Lemuel appeared breathlessly with their saddled animals. John put his index finger to his hat in a gesture of gratitude to the livery man. Quickly, both men swung up, reined on out into the roadway, and swung out in a southerly direction. Once they had cleared town, they boosted their fresh mounts over into a mile-consuming lope.

He thought what John had suggested was entirely possible. So they had not wasted time seeking those two rough-looking drifters in town. As he recalled it, yesterday Rusty Millam had said that Thorne and his hirelings had sat for a long time in the Teton Saloon talking together. Now it seemed to Ethan likely that what they had discussed had been not just part of Thorne's plan, but perhaps all of it, including Thorne's idea of seeking out the northbound stage before it arrived in Winchester. If this were so, then it was very likely those two men were indeed down south somewhere with Thorne right this minute.

But the whole notion was based strictly on conjecture, which is what he now told John, as they sped along through the dazzling morning sunlight.

John's reaction was sanguinary. "We better be right, Ethan. If we aren't, and if DeFore gets his lariat around a couple of necks up in the pass, there'll be enough fireworks around Sherman County for the next few months to last us both a lifetime."

There was no denying the validity of this statement, and Ethan, least of all, would dispute it. But he said: "Any action is better than no action. Furthermore, I don't believe Thorne would have any reason to go up into the pass without a coach, and if he'd tried to take a coach, Hank would have told us when we saw him this morning."

"True," John agreed. Then he smiled ruefully at something that had just come to him. "Hank's been so scared all through this, though, that I think only about half his mind is functioning . . . the scared half."

Southward, beyond Winchester, the valley where the town lay gradually narrowed. Gigantic black peaks and slopes rose up, mostly barren rock and therefore without ground cover. Where the sunlight struck, those great lifts and side-hills gave off a dull reflection. At the base of those gigantic slopes lay a crevice-like pass. In times past this had been a favorite ambushing spot first for Indian warriors, then later on for their successors in the trade of arms—outlaws. But for some years now the Indians had been gone and law enforcement had been so powerfully unrelenting that no trouble had erupted down in that gloomy pass.

Klinger, riding briskly along, considering the onward countryside, said he thought Thorne might try halting the northbound stage in that narrow place. But MacCallister disagreed.

"Too close to town for one thing," he explained, "and if the coach doesn't hit Winchester until noon, it'll be miles south of the pass. No, Thorne's got to make good time. He'll hit the coach somewhere well beyond the pass."

"He'll have to do more than just make good time," John said bleakly. "He'll have to convince that stage-line official that what he's done was a good thing, and I can't see anyone with much sense believing that."

MacCallister put a long look over at his son-in-law. "You never know about people. What makes sense to you and me, makes damned little sense to someone else. Besides, what kind of a company official would send a man like two-gun Ray Thorne up here to settle a dispute in the first place?"

John had no reply for this, so he directed their conversation to a new topic. "Just what does DeFore expect to accomplish with his toll road? He's already wealthy, isn't he?"

"Yeah, he's got all the money he'll ever need."

"Then what's he trying to prove?"

Ethan slowed his horse as they came within good sighting distance of the pass ahead and its darkly forbidding black rock haunches. "DeFore," he said thoughtfully, "is a pretty complex man in a lot of ways. But I don't know. He never told me what he had in mind when he tried to close the pass . . . but I've known him a long time and I've got a guess about that." Ethan looped his reins and began fumbling for his tobacco sack.

"A long time ago, Dick DeFore had a wife and a baby daughter. That was when he was a young man . . . when he first took up land north of what's now Winchester."

"I didn't know that," John said, looking somewhat dumbfounded. "I've never even heard it before."

Ethan struck a match to light up and then blew a geyser of smoke straight ahead. He didn't turn to see his son-in-law staring at him as he resumed speaking.

"Well, there was a bad Indian attack. A massacre I reckon you could call it. That's when the Army moved in. DeFore's young wife and baby daughter were killed. He buried them somewhere up in Cheyenne Pass. I never asked him where and he never told me. In fact, I've never heard him mention his wife and daughter from that day to this, so maybe I'm all wrong about the matter, but I think he wants to keep their burial place a secret. I've sort of figured, since this whole matter commenced, that DeFore wants his shrine . . . or whatever it is up there . . . to remain as it's been since the day he buried his family up there, and that's why he's dead set on making his toll road . . . to keep out people. If he wanted to really close the road, I think he would have said so. But he doesn't, he's just making folks pay to use it, and obviously that'll limit the traffic."

"You don't believe he's out to bankrupt the town?" John asked. "Because that's what I've heard some people saying when DeFore's name comes up around town."

"I've heard that too. But I don't believe that. And I'll tell you something else, I don't believe he really cares whether the stages use that cussed road or not. I think what he's trying to do is stop people from snooping around his land."

John was silent as they rode on down toward the gloomy pass leading out of Winchester Valley to the country to the south. He obviously was digesting what he'd just been told.

They'd gone another mile or so, when he said to Ethan: "I'll say one thing for you old-timers around here. You sure can keep a secret. As long as I've been in this country, I'd never before heard that Richard DeFore had ever been married, let alone had started a family."

Ethan killed his smoke, unlooped his reins, and looked right and left as they entered the pass. In years past he'd charged down into the forbidding place many times after outlaws. Now, in his sundown years, he never entered it without feeling a twinge of uneasiness, apprehension.

As he rode along scanning the slopes on their right and left, he said quietly: "It's not a matter of keeping secrets, son. It's just a matter of there being damned few folks still around who remember back that far, and of those who remember, they respect DeFore's desire not to gossip about something so painful that a man like Dick will never forget as long as he lives."

They entered the pass, the sunlight diminished, and the shadows thickened around them, creating a sinister atmosphere. They travelled for about a half a mile, neither saying a word until they passed out into sunshine again.

Beyond the pass once more, Ethan raised his left arm, pointed far ahead where the land tilted away below them, and said one word: "Dust."

Down where that dust stood up in the crystal-clear, dazzling brightness of this fresh, warm morning, the road angled from west to east as it traced out a course among arroyos and little grassy hills. Far away was another necklace of dark mountains but in between lay a broad, open plain, bowl-shaped, which was gradually depressed toward a central lowlands where trees grew in profusion, and where, through those trees, they could see a silvery sheen from a meandering watercourse. Down here lay some of the richest cattle ranches in Sherman County. Down here too, at one time, had been an ancient Indian gathering ground, called a *rancheria*. There were innumerable faded hieroglyphics painted upon road-side boulders, their meanings entirely lost now, but their presence strongly indicative of another race and another time.

That lazily hanging dust seemed to rise up from the farthest reaches of the stage road. It was much too far for either lawman to make out what was causing it, but Ethan thought it could only be the northbound stage. As soon as he said this, John had another complementing thought to voice.

"If that's the coach, then where is Thorne?"

Ethan nodded toward that central lowlands where the obscuring trees stood. "Probably down there. He'd have a camp, more than likely, and a man doesn't make camp away from water when he doesn't have to." Ethan paused, threw a look off on his left, and reined over in that direction, leaving the road. "I reckon we'd better go sort of carefully from here on. I'd wager Thorne will be having this north route watched."

They passed over into fetlock-high, tough and wiry buffalo grasses, moving eastward until they were easily a mile from the roadway. Then Ethan turned and headed almost due south. He was, John could see, making it a point to keep the bulk of those trees ahead between themselves and whatever might lie beyond the trees.

That dust came closer, but because the distance was so great it did not seem to advance very rapidly. In fact, they got to the first thick stand of cottonwoods near that watercourse they'd seen earlier from up near the black-rock pass, before suddenly the dust seemed no longer to be advancing at all. It seemed to have stopped rising up into the pristine morning air altogether.

Ethan halted in tree shade, strained ahead for a silent moment, then said quietly: "Well, we were right. It's a stage, and a little band of riders have stopped it."

John eased up where he could see what his father-in-law could see, and he grunted his confirmation as he sat as still as Ethan was sitting.

CHAPTER ELEVEN

Without mentioning what he had in mind, MacCallister turned and rode off westerly through the giant old cottonwoods, passing in and out of their mottled, silvery shade until he was within a half mile of the road. There, he halted, got down, stood at his animal's head staring toward the south. When John came up and also dismounted, Ethan said: "No sense in pushing on down there. Let Thorne have his say. I could've wished we'd gotten to that fellow first, but since that was out of the question, I reckon we'll just have to settle for second place."

"You figure to halt the coach?" John asked.

Ethan nodded. "Yeah, we'll stop it. But don't ask me what comes next because I don't know."

For nearly a half hour they stood in the shade before those tiny horsemen far southward swung away, heading eastward in a lope. They watched Thorne and his men to make sure they were not going to change course suddenly, ride north, and perhaps discover that Sherman County's brace of lawmen were also waiting to waylay the same stage.

As soon as it became apparent that Thorne had something else in mind, Ethan relaxed and said: "In a way, I almost hope he does try heading on up into Cheyenne Pass again."

That dust cloud beat upward again and after a while it became possible to make out the vehicle causing it. The coach was one of those Deadwood stages suspended upon thoroughbrace leather springs which gave it a viability found in very few other horse-drawn vehicles, and while this was held firmly by its makers to promote better riding for passengers, there was some vociferous disagreement with this for the basic reason that these coaches did not only rock forward and back upon those leather springs, but the vehicle also rocked from side to side, which made every-one susceptible to seasickness not only uneasy, but sometimes even offensively ill. In fact, as MacCallister and Klinger watched the oncoming stage, they got the definite impression that this particular coach had some additional refinements to it which made it appear to buck and pitch even more than was normal for such vehicles.

John commented upon this, but Ethan's entire concern was upon one passenger in that coach and he said nothing about the lurching and rolling as the vehicle beat on up toward them, scuffing up great gobbets of rearward dust.

When the driver and shotgun guard were discernible at long last, Ethan turned, stepped up, and eased his horse ahead on out of the trees. John followed him and the pair of them passed out into full view.

While they were still a half mile ahead, both lawmen rode to the roadway's center and drew rein. They had been sighted of course and the driver, along with the shotgun guard upon the overhead seat, seemed stiffly wary and very alert.

MacCallister raised his left arm to halt the coach. It slowed, the horses broke over from their easy lope to a slamming trot, and the noise of harness and coach both, increased as it drew closer.

The badges of both MacCallister and Klinger were in plain sight upon their shirt fronts. Evidently the two wary coach men upon the high seat had caught reflections from those symbols of local authority, for they seemed to slacken away from their former stiffness as the horses slowed again, coming down to a fast walk.

MacCallister waited until the driver set his brake before reining out of the roadway, passing along beside the teams, and halting with John at his side, near the fore-wheel. A great, shaggy head poked itself out of a side window and bawled up at the driver. Two fierce eyes in a very fat, moon-shaped face suddenly saw Ethan and John, saw the badges, and that massive passenger abruptly closed his mouth and withdrew his head.

A second later the coach lurched, the door was flung back, and an imposing fat man stepped out. He was attired in the clothing of a big-city dweller. Despite enormous crescents at each armpit and wildly flowing curly hair, this man exuded authority. As Klinger regarded this stranger he had his answer to why the coach had been listing and plunging so noticeably as it beat its way up the road. That fat man had to weigh three hundred pounds if he weighed an ounce.

MacCallister also considered the passenger. He made no move to dismount as he stared, and when that huge man started forward, balancing upon the balls of his feet, the deputy was surprised at the ease of his movements. He wasn't all fat; somewhere under all that meat was a powerful set of muscles.

The big man halted, shaded his eyes from sunlight, and stood a moment, staring first at MacCallister, then on over at Klinger. Finally he dropped his shading hand, scowled darkly, and said: "Just exactly what is the meaning of this?" He was indignant. More than that, he was antagonistic.

Ethan sighed. Evidently Thorne had done his work well.

"Mister," John began, "my name is Klinger. John Klinger. I'm sheriff of Sherman County. This here is Ethan MacCallister, my deputy. Are you the stage-line executive who wired that he was coming up to Winchester?"

"I am!" barked the big man, abruptly inclining his leonine head. "The name is Charles Mather.

Now will you men tell me why you stopped this stage?"

"Sure," John replied in a quiet voice. "Be glad to. Because we want to know if you're the one responsible for sending Ray Thorne to Winchester."

"I am. What of that?"

"Did you know who Thorne was when you hired him?"

Charles Mather fisted a handkerchief, made a quick swipe at his perspiring face with it, then dropped the hand, still with the handkerchief in it and squinted truculently up at the sheriff.

"If you mean did I know Ray Thorne was a doer instead of a talker . . . yes, I knew that. Why else would I have sent him here?"

"More than just a doer, Mister Mather," MacCallister informed him. "A killer. When he stopped your coach down the road a while back, did he tell you he sent two men up to Cheyenne Pass with dynamite to force a fight last night?"

"Deputy," exclaimed the copiously perspiring fat man, "what stage company employees tell me in confidence goes no further."

"In that case," shot back MacCallister, "I reckon we'd better make you a proposition, Mister Mather."

"What proposition?" the fat man shouted as he glared.

"You talk, or you go to jail," MacCallister

129

stated evenly, and leaned back in his saddle, crossed both hands upon his saddle horn, and gave Charles Mather as hard a stare as Mather threw out at Ethan.

"This is an outrage," sputtered Mather. "What authority have you to . . . ?"

"Rope it," MacCallister snapped flintily. "We're not going to sit out here and argue with you all day, Mather. What did you and Ray Thorne cook up when he stopped this stage an hour or so ago?"

"We didn't cook up anything. He simply made his report to me."

"And what did he report?"

"That this man Richard DeFore . . . and the local law . . . twice circumvented our coaches from rolling up through Cheyenne Pass, and that he now has hired some riders to go out with the next coach to make certain that it gets through. He also told me the law in Winchester County is hand-in-glove with this DeFore person, probably for the purpose of extorting money from the stage company. Does that suit you, Deputy?"

"Suits me fine," replied MacCallister, glancing over at John.

The sheriff nodded and fixed Mather with a wintry gaze. "It suits me fine as well," Klinger said, "because all we wanted to be sure of is that Thorne is a complete liar and that you mean to back him up in forcing a war on the county."

"Forcing a war," the indignant stage-line official roared. "Who closed this Cheyenne Pass in the first place? Who sent his crew out to ambush two of our riders last night? Who is trying to force this company to pay money for using a public thoroughfare?"

"Mister," Klinger replied coldly now, "in the first place, Cheyenne Pass is not a dedicated road and as far as I know it never has been. In the second place, no one ambushed Thorne's men last night . . . but they shot Richard DeFore's foreman, and we've got the dynamite they were carrying in our office in town right now." He paused to suck back a big breath before going on. "And finally, I've never heard DeFore or anyone except Thorne mention extortion of money from your stage line."

"Haven't you now," ranted the fat man. "What do you think a toll road is, if it's not an attempt at extortion?"

MacCallister cut in here: "Mister Mather, you're a fool if you believe Ray Thorne. That man's reputation is notorious. You're also a bigger fool if you believe half of what he's told you. And you may wind up a dead fool if you arrive in Winchester today breathing fire and brimstone like you're doing now, because this morning Richard DeFore rode into town fired up for a fight. Now I know that maybe that doesn't mean much to you, but take it from me, DeFore eats fellows like you for breakfast, when he's roiled up."

"Hah!" the big man guffawed. "I see that Thorne didn't lie about one thing. The law hereabouts is on DeFore's side. Well, gentlemen, let me tell you something. I've come here with a free hand from the president and vice-president of the company. I also came here with an open checkbook. If DeFore wants a fight, I can personally guarantee him one. Thorne said all we need is money to hire fighters, and I have brought that money."

The fat man whipped back around, reached for the stage door, and lightly got back inside. As he seated himself, he leaned forward to slam the door closed, at the same time that MacCallister eased up his horse, put out a hand to hold the door open. He looked down into Mather's sweat-shiny and angry-eyed countenance.

He said: "Mister Mather, have you ever been under arrest before?"

Those angry eyes clouded. "Before . . . ?"

"Yes, Mister Mather . . . before. Because, you see, you're under arrest now."

MacCallister gave the stage door a hard slam, whirled his horse, and halted beside the fore-wheel again. As Mather's leonine head came thrusting through the window behind him, the deputy sheriff said: "Driver, head out. We'll ride on each side of your coach. Don't head for the stage office when you get into Winchester. Stop a half block south of the office at the county jailhouse. And driver . . ."—Ethan smiled upward coldly—"don't do anything foolish, because we've got plenty of empty cells this time of year."

The driver shook his head. "No," he said, "I won't do anything foolish." He rolled his eyes as Charles Mather let off a string of furious profanity from within the coach.

The two lawmen split up when the coach began rolling forward, one on either side as the vehicle gained speed and momentum. Once or twice they exchanged sober looks, but mostly they galloped along thinking their private thoughts.

It was afternoon by the time Winchester came into sight beyond the black-rock pass. By the time the coach hit Winchester's outskirts and the driver slowed his horses, both Ethan and John were mantled with the dust the vehicle they had accompanied had stirred up. People upon the walkways turned to look, then halted to stand, mouths agape, as the stage wheeled in at the jailhouse and creaked down to a halt. Up the roadway Hank Weaver was standing in front of his office, green eye-shade on, clipboard in hand, looking nonplussed.

MacCallister swung down, jerked open the door, and motioned for Charles Mather to alight.

The fat man did, but as he turned his fiery red face upon Ethan, John came up and cut across the fat man's forming words with a curt order.

"Inside . . . and shut up!"

Mather's mouth snapped closed. He looked straight at the sheriff, saw nothing but toughness and willingness in John's face, and stalked on around the coach. As he moved out, John fell in behind him, herding Mather into his office.

MacCallister stepped along to where he could see the driver, and affably said: "Thanks, son. You were right cooperative. Now you'd better take the coach on up where that fellow with the eye-shade is standing, because he's about to burst with questions." Then he stepped away.

The coach lurched on toward the stage office, and after it had passed, MacCallister took his and John's horses, walked up through the roadway dust as far as the livery barn, and left the animals there with Lemuel. He then headed back toward the jailhouse, and, in so doing, was obliged to pass the spot where a little cluster of men were crowded up around Hank Weaver and the driver who'd tooled Charles Mather's stage into town.

He would have marched past without speaking, but Clem Whipple stopped him. "Ethan, for Pete's sake what's goin' on?"

"Don't worry, Clem," Ethan said dismissively, and continued on by.

"Don't worry!" Clem exclaimed shrilly, as he

ran as best he could, trying to keep up with the deputy. "Haven't you heard . . . old man DeFore's been back in town? He's over at the telegraph office right now, and folks are sayin' he's wired for a whole damned army of gunfighters to come up here and join him in bustin' the stage line."

Ethan's stomach knotted up. He stared at Clem, at gray-faced Weaver, and at the other townsmen standing there with them. Two of those men— one Dr. Shirley and the other man Winchester's most prominent hotel and saloon owner—looked gravely at Ethan and inclined their heads.

"It's true, Deputy," said the doctor. "When DeFore stopped in to see how Browne was getting along, he told me he was going to teach those stage company hotshots down in Denver a lesson they'd never forget."

MacCallister turned away, his face frozen, and continued on his way toward the jailhouse.

CHAPTER TWELVE

Sheriff Klinger had Charles Mather booked and locked up by the time Ethan returned. He was examining a little pearl-handled under-and-over .41-caliber pistol when Ethan walked in. He held the gun up for Ethan to see.

"Took it off Mather," John said. "Two shots, then you're all through."

"Never mind that," Ethan said. "Come on over to the telegraph office with me."

There was something in his father-in-law's face that drew the sheriff abruptly out of his chair. Without a word he put down the little double-barreled gun and followed Ethan back out into the roadway. The pair of them hiked straight over to the telegraph office, and, there, Ethan said to the telegrapher: "Al, I know it's against the rules, but I've got to see the copy of that wire Richard DeFore sent."

The telegrapher said nothing. He offered no excuses and no arguments. He simply picked up a yellow slip of paper and placed it squarely in front of MacCallister upon the counter. He stood there as the two lawmen read it. When they looked up, he told them: "I was going to fetch it over as soon as I knew you fellows were back in town."

John poked a finger at the name of the man to whom that telegram was addressed and said to Ethan: "Who's he . . . some special gunslinger?"

"He," pronounced Ethan, "is the man who recruited the gunmen for Wyoming's cattlemen in the Johnson County War."

Ethan stood a moment in frowning concentration, then he faced the telegrapher, regarded him skeptically a moment, asked for a pencil, and turned DeFore's telegram over. He began to write a message upon the back of it. When he finished, he handed back the pencil, slid the paper over, and tapped it.

"Send this to the same man," he instructed the telegrapher. "It tells him there has been a settlement of differences here in Sherman County and he won't have to recruit the gunfighters after all."

The telegrapher read what Ethan had written and nodded. He raised amused eyes and said: "Ethan, whose signature do I put . . . DeFore's?"

Ethan met that little whimsical smile with a bleak and humorless grin of his own. "Yeah, Richard DeFore's name. A man might as well get hung for a lion as a sheep. Since I've got to be a liar, I might as well be a big one."

MacCallister put a silver dollar upon the counter and led his son-in-law back out into the roadway. Here and there, in front of the store fronts, men stood in little groups talking. Over in front of the stage office where Hank Weaver, Clem Whipple, and several others stood, Ethan saw the lank form of Weaver disengage itself from the others and start resolutely southward. He sighed.

"Hurry it up, John. Hank's trying to catch up with us. No doubt he wants to let us know his feelings about us halting the stage and arresting his boss."

They returned to the jailhouse and arrived at the doorway just as Weaver came up. The stage-line manager furrowed his brow into a series of deep rolls and ridges. He stepped on inside as Ethan beckoned him to, then, when the three of them were in the office, Hank did exactly as Ethan had prophesied.

"I think I know what you're trying to do," Weaver said in a squeaky voice, his eyes twitching nervously at the two lawmen, "but if you keep Mister Mather locked up, it's only going to make things worse."

"How can it make things worse?" John grumbled as he stepped over to the stove to get the fire going for coffee. "Thorne stopped the stage and filled Mather full of lies." John poked in the ashes, found some hot coals, and carefully placed kindling atop them as his father-in-law came over with the coffee pot.

Ethan said soothingly: "Just keep out of it,

Hank, and you'll likely live to be a very old man."

"But Mister Mather is one of the top men in the company, Ethan. Doesn't that mean anything? I mean, he's not the type to make trouble and . . ."

"Hank," John said, straightening around. "How well do you know Charles Mather?"

"Well, we've never actually met, you see, but for him to be treated . . ."

"Let me tell you something. Bigwigs make mistakes, too, just like us common folks, and your Mister Mather's human. Now go on back to the stage office and keep out of this. It's complicated enough without you butting in."

Weaver's eyes squinted closed, popped wide open, and squinted nearly closed again. He and John exchanged a long look at one another. Finally Weaver moved over to the door, but before he departed, he said: "I got to make a report of this to the Denver office. It's my duty. Besides, they'll want to know."

"Well now, you do what you've got to do," said John, "and leave the law end of this thing to us."

After Weaver left, Ethan turned an approving look upon his son-in-law. "Handled it just right," he said. "No temper, no cussing, just the plain facts of life. You're coming along nicely, John." He paused, then said: "Can you handle DeFore as well?"

"DeFore?"

"Sure, we've got to get to him next. With Mather taken care of and with Thorne running loose somewhere, we've got to get to DeFore before he runs across Thorne and there's a lot of killing."

"Why not Thorne? He's the one we ought to run down next, isn't he?"

"Sure he is, but we don't know where he went after stopping the stage, and if we waste a lot of time trying to find him, all we'll accomplish is a big, fat lot of nothing. So, the alternative is to get to DeFore and try to stop him first."

John considered this as the little stove crackled merrily. He eventually nodded his head, went over to the gun rack, selected a shotgun, and stuffed a handful of shotgun shells into a pocket. As he faced back around, Ethan shook his head.

"You won't need that thing. I know Dick DeFore well enough to believe, while he may never see eye to eye with us, he sure wouldn't encourage his men to shoot it out with the law."

John hefted the shotgun, shrugged, and put it back in the rack. He neglected to empty the shells from his pocket because at that moment the roadside door opened, the doctor stepped through, and John's thoughts were scattered by what the medical man said.

"Sheriff . . . Deputy. Travis Browne is getting ready to leave."

MacCallister stood like stone staring over

toward the door. "Leaving? What are you talking about? He's got a busted arm, some cracked ribs, and a dented skull. How can he be leaving?"

Dr. Shirley put a sardonic glance upon Ethan. "He's getting dressed right now . . . one-handed. When I tried to stop him, he told me not to interfere, that he was going back to the DeFore place to join the hunt for Thorne and Thorne's crew."

Incredulously, John said: "Can he ride, Doctor?"

"If he can get astraddle of a horse, he can ride. So, my answer is yes, Sheriff. But how far he can ride before he passes out is another question."

"Fine," the deputy mumbled, and cursed under his breath. "Well, come on, John. There's only one thing to do."

The doctor did not remove himself from in front of the door as the two peace officers advanced upon him. "What are you going to do?" he asked. "Listen to me. Mister DeFore left a pistol with Browne and remember, gentlemen, it's his left arm that's broken, not his right. He's very determined about this. If you walk in there to stop him, someone is going to get hurt."

Ethan smiled frostily, put his head a little to one side, and said: "Doc, you stick to healing and we'll stick to lawing. All right? Come on, John, the damned coffee will have to wait."

They passed out into the afternoon heat, swung northward, and went along, side-by-side, as far as the livery barn. There, where Lemuel Sinclair, was sitting in the shade just inside his doorway, idly watching the roadway, Ethan paused long enough to say: "Lemuel, don't let Travis Browne have a horse if he comes down here to hire one. You understand?"

Lemuel lifted round eyes. "I understand, but Travis is laid up, isn't he? Folks say he's shot-up a little or something . . . staying at Doc's place."

"He doesn't think he's hurt and he may try to hire a horse from you. See to it that he doesn't get one."

"Sure, Ethan, sure. I promise he won't get one."

The lawmen moved off again, and Lemuel joined several dozen other interested spectators the length of Winchester's main roadway who watched their progress with considerable interest and bare-faced curiosity. By now, thanks to Hank Weaver, the stage driver who came in from Denver, as well as a few others, Winchester's citizens had a fair idea of what was in progress. What they didn't actually know, they glibly invented—a prerogative of people the world over.

When Ethan MacCallister and John Klinger walked into the doctor's house, they were stopped dead in their tracks by a six-gun held in the steady right hand of a grim-faced Travis Browne.

"I figured Sinclair would do something like

this," Browne told the lawmen. "He's the type."

Browne was fully clothed and his hat sat balanced atop his bandaged head. He seemed perfectly all right. His eyes were clear, and while he breathed very shallowly so as to minimize the pain from his damaged ribs, he looked and acted both fit and determined. One thing in particular held the attention of the lawmen—that loaded six-gun didn't waver one iota.

"You'll never make it," said John. "Travis, take my advice and . . ."

"Advice from you, John Klinger, is the last thing in this world I'll ever take," snarled Browne.

Ethan eased off. He stepped over to a chair in the doctor's small side room, sat down over there, and picked up a newspaper which he began to examine cursorily as he said in a casual tone of voice: "Put up the gun, Travis. You're not going anywhere." He looked over the newspaper's uppermost edge. "You see, we brought along some men and stationed them outside . . . just in case." Ethan flicked the paper, lowered it a little, and while he scanned its headlines, he said in the same indifferent manner: "And down at the livery barn we've already fixed it so's you can't get a horse."

Browne considered Ethan suspiciously. He did not put up the gun though. In fact he didn't even lower it. He swung his attention back to Klinger, drew back a short breath, and growled: "John, you're going to walk out of here ahead of me. Then we'll see whether I get a horse or not."

Now Ethan said, very gently: "Travis, shoot or put up the gun." He moved his newspaper just enough for both Browne and his son-in-law to see the barrel of his fisted .45 trained unerringly upon Browne's middle. As he put the newspaper aside on a small table, he said: "Never was one to read much, but twenty years ago I first saw this trick pulled, and it's a pretty good one."

Browne's knuckles whitened around his gun. His eyes blazed with silent fury. For a moment it seemed that he might shoot.

"Stand-off," MacCallister warned, his eyes got small and deadly calm. "But you've got to know the odds favor me."

"Do they?" Browne murmured in the same soft tone of voice. "You sure of that, Ethan?"

"Plumb sure, Travis. DeFore wouldn't want any of his men to shoot it out with the law. That would make not only you, but him, too, fugitives and outlaws. But with me it's different. I'll shoot, Travis, don't make any mistake about that. I never bluffed in my life and I'm not bluffing now. I'll break your arm or shoot you in the leg. I won't kill you, but I'll sure fix it so you'll be spending a goodly stretch of time in bed on your back."

Browne licked his lips, shifted his grip on

145

the six-gun, looked at Klinger, and back at MacCallister again. He had a decision to make. One that would indubitably affect the rest of his life because the shooting of a lawman in the performance of his duty was a crime that was never excused. It was a one-sided decision in more ways than one. Klinger was fast and accurate with a gun. If Travis shot John's father-in-law, whether he hit him or not, he wouldn't have time to swing and face Klinger, who would most certainly go into action at the first explosion. Either way, Browne had a decision to make, and if he made the wrong one, he probably would die right where he stood, if not from Ethan's gun, then from Ethan's son-in-law's gun.

Browne let his gun hand sag. He expelled a rattling breath. He said, with no particular animosity in his voice: "Damn you, Ethan MacCallister."

John stepped over, took the gun from Browne's hand, and pushed it into his waistband. His face was white and his eyes were twice as dark as they normally were.

Ethan got up, holstered his weapon, and jerked his head. "Walk on out with us," he ordered Browne.

"Where to?"

"The jailhouse. You're getting well too fast. We've got to go find DeFore and I figure the safest place for you until we get back is the jailhouse."

Browne took one step, halted, and said: "One of you go out first. I don't want those fellows out there opening up when they see me coming out."

"What fellows?" Ethan asked, and slowly smiled. "I lied to you, Travis, but I won't apologize for it. If a little lie is necessary to save a man's life, I'm willing to lie. Go on now."

The three of them emerged from the doctor's house, and at once it was apparent that someone—probably the doctor himself—had warned those interested townsmen out in the roadway what was going on, because, while dozens of faces were peering at the house, mostly it was from within stores and recessed doorways.

The three of them marched grimly down to the jailhouse. No one accosted or interfered with them on the way.

When they entered, Ethan wrinkled his nose. The coffee was aromatically boiling.

CHAPTER THIRTEEN

Travis Browne had a cup of coffee with the sheriff and deputy sheriff. He sipped it, made a wry face over its hot bitterness, and said impatiently: "Don't you fellows ever scrub out that coffee pot?"

MacCallister smiled but Klinger turned his back on the prisoner. He and Browne still scrupulously observed their private feud. John refused to forget that Travis had tried to win his wife before Ruth and he were married, and Travis, perhaps with more justification, declined to be magnanimous toward John, the winner in that amorous pursuit.

"Where'll we find DeFore?" MacCallister asked of Browne, adding when he saw hesitancy in his eyes: "Listen, Travis, you might as well tell us, because if we don't find him, Ray Thorne might get to him first. You don't want that to happen and neither do we, so give us a little help in this."

"Thorne!" Browne spat out. "What can that tinhorn and those two hirelings of his do against Mister DeFore and five damned good cowboys?"

"Four hirelings, not two, Travis, and counting Thorne . . . who's no tinhorn . . . that evens up the sides," Ethan informed him. "And furthermore,

Thorne knows what he's doing, which is more than I can say for your boss."

"What do you mean by that?" demanded Browne, bristling.

"Thorne is up to something. He's got the two men you fellows chased out of the pass last night with him. From now on he'll be as elusive as a greased snake and five times as deadly. He'll know DeFore is hunting him by now and he'll know DeFore is somewhere up near the pass . . . on DeFore's own range. Now, Travis, if you don't think that adds up to bad trouble, you're crazy."

"All right. It adds up to bad trouble. What do you want me to do about it . . . locked up in your lousy jail?"

"Tell us about where DeFore might be and save us a lot of unnecessary riding, because if I've got this thing figured out right, Thorne is now out to kill Dick DeFore."

"Kill him?"

"Yes, kill him. How else can Thorne force a passage for the stagecoaches up through Cheyenne Pass? How else can he hope to collect a big fee for fixing things for the stage line?"

Browne looked over as Klinger turned back to face him. The two exchanged their usual look of unrelenting animosity, then Browne swung back toward MacCallister.

"I got no idea where the boss would look for

Thorne, but I can tell you this . . . he'll be north of the pass, because he's always said that the best place to stop the coaches was north about a mile where the trace is rutted and the stages always have to slow to a walk."

Ethan got up, motioned for Browne to stand up, and pointed toward the cell-block door. He said to his son-in-law: "John, I'll go get us a couple of fresh horses. You lock Travis up. Put him in the cell next to Mather."

As Ethan walked out, John herded their second prisoner of the day toward the cell-block. Of course Browne remained colder toward the sheriff than he'd been toward the deputy, and once he was locked in a cell adjoining Mather's, he turned, leaned upon the bars, and said stonily: "Klinger, if it'd been you who pulled that sneaky trick on me at the doctor's place, I'd have drawn against you."

John finished locking the cell door, shrugged, and started to turn away.

Charles Mather snapped at him, bringing the sheriff back around.

He said: "I'm going to have the badges off both you and your deputy for this outrage, Sheriff. I swear to you I will."

Slowly Browne turned to gaze through the bars at his fellow prisoner. He said: "Just who are you, mister?"

Mather swung his glare to encompass Browne.

151

"An official of the stage line, if it's any of your business, cowboy."

Browne stood staring for a long time. "In case you're interested," he eventually said, "I'm Travis Browne . . . range boss for Richard DeFore, the man who says you stage people got to pay a toll to use Cheyenne Pass."

Mather's fiery gaze swung away from the sheriff, fastened itself upon Browne, and made a slow, careful study of the cowboy, at the same time losing some of its fierce rancor. Finally Mather said: "Is that so? And just what the devil are you doing locked up too? I was informed the law is on your side."

Browne snorted, shot a sulphurous look out at John, and shook his head. "Mister, I don't know who told you that, but I'll tell you one thing . . . he sure didn't know what he was talking about."

John, watching the big fat man, saw Mather's eyes lose all their anger and become perplexed as he gradually made a faint frown over at Browne.

"Ray Thorne told me that," Mather said.

This time Browne's snort was unmistakably derisive. "And you believed that tinhorn gunslinger?" he cried. "Well, mister, you're as green as grass if you believe what a man like Ray Thorne tells you. Hell, the law in these parts doesn't take sides. It never has, and while I got no more use for these here lawmen than you probably have, I'll tell you one thing . . . you can't buy 'em and neither can my boss."

John, hearing a commotion in the outer office, turned and walked on out there. He closed and carefully bolted the cell-block door, straightened around expecting to see Ethan standing there, but instead saw Weaver and two strangers.

While John was considering the two strangers, Weaver said: "Sheriff, these here fellows are from a mine back in the mountains that ships its refined bar gold to the Denver mint on our stages. They come ahead each time to make the arrangements, only this time I had to tell 'em the stages were having a little trouble, so they wanted to talk to you."

"No trouble going south," John said to the two strangers. "Only going north. Cheyenne Pass is closed."

Out in the roadway, MacCallister's recognizable voice called out. John stepped forward, nodded briskly at the men, opened the door, and passed on out, leaving Weaver and the mine men behind in the office.

As he stepped up beside John, he told his father-in-law about the two mine men Weaver had brought to see him.

MacCallister seemed uninterested as he commented. "Yeah, they've been operating like that for about five years. The mine sends a couple of bully boys on ahead to see that everything is all right, then one of them returns, rides back to town with the bullion cart, and the two of them get on the stage with the gold and head down to Denver. It's pure routine."

Klinger concentrated upon riding along beside Ethan on the northward road. The land was still and burnished to a soft afternoon bronze. The road was empty as far as they could see. While still several miles below the uplands Ethan suggested that they ride off parallel to the road instead of upon it, because he thought it likely that one faction or the other, or perhaps both, would have sentinels somewhere up ahead keeping watch.

They passed around the slope of a grassy hill-side, entered the broken northward hills in this way, and came close to the abrupt drop-off where they'd found Travis Browne. Here, they halted to rest their animals.

As he dismounted, MacCallister said: "You know, a man gets used to a lot of inconvenience in this line of work, but there's one thing he never gets used to . . . being hungry."

John smiled, took in the roundabout hills and slopes with an inquiring glance, then dismounted and walked up where his father-in-law stood, fully exposed and making a cigarette. He said: "Wouldn't it be better to get out of sight and into the shade?"

Ethan finished building his cigarette, inspected it, popped it between his lips. He struck a match along the seat of his trousers as he answered. "Too late for that, son." He inhaled, exhaled, removed the smoke, and looked casually up the side-hill on their right. He didn't say a word, he didn't have to.

John's eyes caught what Ethan saw—two horsemen sitting their horses up against the reddening sky and watching them. He grunted: "How long they been up there?"

Ethan inhaled, exhaled, and turned toward his animal. "Not very long . . . just since we stopped. But they been trailing us for the past half hour, ever since we cut around into the hills from the roadway." Ethan mounted, settled himself, and looked down. "Might as well ride on up and palaver with 'em. Otherwise, they're going to keep on skulking along behind us."

John mounted and turned to follow Ethan up the slope. As he did this, he said: "DeFore's men or Thorne's?"

"DeFore's," Ethan replied, concentrating on helping his horse find the easiest route uphill.

Above, those two saddled men sat like statues, watching, motionless, and totally silent. Behind them stood a cloud castle in the dying day, its edges red-encrusted and its backgrounding expanse of sky a soft pink. Elsewhere, south and north, the land was tilted and sloping, but directly behind those two cowboys, a little more than a mile, lay the deserted flow of the trace through Cheyenne Pass.

When Ethan was close enough to make sure he would be heard and understood, he called ahead to the sentinels. "You boys would make fair Indians," he said. " 'Course, no self-respecting Indian would skyline himself like you fellows are doing now."

One of those men sang back: "Well now, Sheriff, I reckon if an Indian wanted to be noticed, he'd skyline himself wouldn't he?"

Ethan halted his horse a hundred feet out, twisted to watch John come up the last hundred yards, then straightened forward to study the two DeFore riders. He knew them both, not personally but casually.

"If you wanted to be noticed, son," he said to one of the men sitting grave-faced and watching apprehensively, "you could've sung out when you first commenced trailing us a mile back down near the flat country."

The second cowboy looked over at his companion and chuckled. To Ethan this one said: "Hell, Deputy, you just dealt his pride a plumb mortal blow. He's been telling me all the while we been tagging you fellows how good a scout he was."

Ethan's eyes twinkled. "Maybe he'll also tell

me where Mister DeFore is, if he's in a talkative mood."

The unsmiling cowboy nodded. "I can do better than that, Sheriff . . . I'll take you to him. Sort of figured on doing that anyway. By invitation of course . . . you understand, wouldn't neither one of us think of coercing officers of the law."

The two DeFore riders turned and struck out due east for the stage road, but just before they came to it, they swung north and skirted around several up-ended granite slopes.

It was a long ride and a slow one. In this eroded, broken upland country no prudent man pushed a horse, the air being thin and the footing treacherous. But before sunset the two cowboys drew rein at the base of a little plateau and pointed out a side-hill trail that wound upward toward an overhead spot.

"Hit that trail and stay on it, Sheriff. Mister DeFore is up there."

Ethan said: "You two aren't coming?"

"Nope. Our orders are to spot trespassers. You two fellows are different. We figure Mister DeFore will want to see you. But anyone else . . . no dice. Our orders are to run 'em off."

As the cowboys were reining around, John called after them: "What about Thorne . . . did you see any trace of him?"

One of the DeFore men twisted in the saddle, shook his head, and kept on riding.

The onward trail was a good one. It was wide and not too steep. In considering it now, MacCallister had a sudden idea that this trail was kept brushed off and open for some definite purpose. He led out without a word and John followed.

They climbed steadily toward the overhead plateau and Ethan racked his brain to recall whether he'd ever before visited this particular mesa. He was certain, after a while, that he had not, then John made an observation that set Ethan to thinking again.

"Ethan, this trail isn't visible from the stage road."

Ethan saw at once that it wasn't. But he said nothing until they were near the top out.

"You can see the whole blessed countryside from up here, John. I'll bet you there used to be one of those old Indian watchtowers up here."

But that wasn't what Ethan was thinking about at all.

They made the last big turn, climbed a steep hundred feet, and emerged upon the absolutely flat top of a mesa. There were several trees upon this wind-swept, silent, lost world of soft grass and endless wildflowers. There was also a stone chapel. At least to Ethan it looked like a chapel—the roof was gabled, very peaked, and slate-covered. The walls were made of carefully squared and mortared fieldstone. There were two little glass windows in this unique little building which caught and reflected the setting sun, throwing back a bronze light.

John dropped his rein hand and whispered: "I'll be damned."

Ethan sat looking, saying nothing. Finally, when a horseman came around the little stone chapel, heading over toward them, Ethan commented: "Son, I think we've just discovered something only DeFore and his men have known about."

"I agree," John breathed. "Probably the burial grounds of Richard DeFore. Ethan, how did he ever manage to keep it a secret this long?"

"Easy, son, easy. Think back over the riders you've known that he hired. Men like Travis Browne and those two that brought us here. That's why he hired only men he could trust. Men willing to keep his secret and maintain this place. I told you, Dick DeFore's a complex man."

"The rider's beckoning to us, Ethan."

"Yeah. Let's go."

They rode slowly across toward that solemn little chapel, and a big, raw-boned man emerged from it to watch them and await their arrival.

CHAPTER FOURTEEN

Richard DeFore's weathered face was smoothed over and unreadable as Ethan and his son-in-law halted twenty feet away and sat their saddles in long silence. The cowman made a hand motion to the rider sitting off to one side at which the cowboy reversed his animal, riding on around the little stone building.

DeFore ignored John and spoke directly to Ethan, with all the customary roughness absent from his voice.

"Never been up here before, have you, Ethan?"

"No," replied MacCallister, "I never have."

"All right, get down, both of you."

Ethan swung down. So did John. They stood at their horses' heads, holding their reins. DeFore kept watching them both, his face expressionless. After a moment he said: "Ethan, you're an old-timer. You'll remember things from many years back, things other folks have all but forgotten. Things the newcomers like your son-in-law here never heard at all."

"Well," Ethan said evenly, "I told him a few things, Dick."

"You did?"

"Yeah."

"Are we talking about the same things, Ethan?"

"I reckon we are, Dick." Ethan made a gesture roundabout with his left hand. "I've never been up here before, never had a reason for looking for any such place. But I knew it'd be somewhere close by."

DeFore faintly inclined his head. "Yeah. That's how it is with old-timers," he said. "They know. They remember. But they don't go poking and prying like newcomers do."

DeFore turned from the waist, gestured toward the little fieldstone chapel, and straightened back around. His expression was readable now; it was full of iron determination and stubborn willfulness.

"I've seen 'em on the pass, Ethan. They get off the stage when the horses are being rested up. They go walking around, looking in places they have no business looking, leaving their garbage around, smoking their stinking cigars. I know sooner or later they'd find this place. They'd leave their filth up here, too."

"Fence it off, Dick."

"Fence it off," growled the old cowman bitterly. "What good do fences do? They keep cattle and horses out . . . sometimes. But they only invite curiosity in people. Anyway, Ethan, this is my land, every square foot of it. When I want to keep snoopers out, I got that right."

The old cowman was glaring fiercely now and Ethan stood silently, returning his stare, waiting for that wintry storm to pass, determined to say nothing, to do nothing, which might feed DeFore's ire.

"That means the stages in particular," DeFore hissed. "They'll pay my toll or they won't come through this way."

"It's the only pass, Dick. You know that. The alternative is four miles west of here."

"Then let 'em use the alternate route. I don't care. I don't want 'em stumbling up in here anyway."

"Even if they didn't stop, Dick?"

"They *do* stop, Ethan. I've sat up here and watched 'em stop. It's their custom."

"It's not so much their custom, Dick, as it's a plain necessity. They have to blow the teams. That's quite a climb from the south slope. You know that."

"I'm not arguing about what they have to do. I'm stating what they're going to do."

"But, hell, Dick, making them pay a toll . . . making everyone who comes through here pay a toll . . . isn't going to change anything. Sure, it may discourage some travelers, but not the stages, and they seem to be your particular gripe."

"My toll," ground out the older man, "will let folks know they got no rights in this pass, Ethan. It'll let 'em know they'd better not loiter around up in here."

As Ethan started to speak again, DeFore flung up an arm. He half twisted to see what the rider wanted who came around from behind the little stone chapel. At once DeFore was different. He was no longer argumentative or bitter, but became now coldly calculating and aggressive.

The rider said: "Horsemen comin' in from the east, Mister DeFore. From over in the direction of the home place."

"How many?"

"Five," replied the cowboy.

Ethan made an inaudible sigh at that one word. The only five riders he knew of who would be scouting through the hills instead of frontally approaching Cheyenne Pass, would be Ray Thorne and his four riders.

"All right," the old cowman said briskly. "Go on down and warn the others, then all of you take positions where you can keep an eye on 'em. Once you determine that this is that two-gun man the stage line hired, let me know at once."

As the cowboy whirled to ride off, DeFore whipped back around to face Ethan and John.

"All I wanted was to protect what's sacred to me, Ethan. That's all. And what do I get for doing that? A damned war pushed on me by the stage company. Well, if that's what those Denver whelps want, they'll damned well get it! I sent for more guns."

"No," Ethan informed DeFore. "I counter-

164

manded that, Dick. I sent a telegram, too. There'll be no more gunmen come into my county. Not for you and not for the stage line. As for those big executives down in Denver . . . John and I stopped the northbound stage this morning and arrested one of them. He's locked in the jailhouse back in town right this minute."

These statements seemed to jar the old cowman. At first he seemed to bristle with wrath at Ethan's interference in his hiring more gunmen, then he stared as Ethan told of locking up Charles Mather. Finally, he shuffled his feet, looked out over the shadowing land, declaring: "Ethan, you had no right to interfere."

But most of the fire was gone from his voice.

"I had every right," contradicted MacCallister. "My job's to keep the peace. I aim to do exactly that. Incidentally, Travis tried to leave town and join you. I locked him up along with Mather."

This brought DeFore's hawk-like stare sharply around. "Travis? He's hurt! He couldn't get up here by himself."

"He thought he could. At least he was willing to try it. And if he's hurt, by golly, he's tougher than a boiled owl, because he threw down on me with that six-gun you left him, Dick."

"The hell he did."

Ethan nodded. "Travis is a good man. Maybe in his boots I'd have done the same. Anyway, we had to lock him up."

Old Richard DeFore lapsed into a long silence. When he eventually emerged from it, he said: "I built this little chapel myself. Built the road up here, too . . . around the back way so no one could see it from the stage road. My wife and daughter are buried behind the chapel. Everything I'm doing now is in their honor, to protect their memory." DeFore stopped speaking, looked steadily over at John before continuing.

"Ethan, your girl grew up. I used to see her down in town. I used to figure my girl would be just about like her . . . same age, same size and coloring. You know, I've often thought, if things had been different, my girl would have grown up and maybe married young Travis. He's like a son to me. I reckon you can understand that, Ethan."

"I can understand it, Dick."

"Well, that's why I never wanted much truck with you. Your girl lived and grew up and married. Someday you'll have a grandson."

Ethan sighed before he said with sudden intensity: "Dick, you listen to me. Coming up to this place . . . spending so much time at this chapel with those two graves . . . is going to warp you. It's already upset your judgement to the extent that you're trying to make the whole world pay for crossing through Cheyenne Pass. I can tell you, Travis will meet the right girl one of these days. He'll get married and live on the ranch, and someday he'll even give you a grandson, being that he's the same as a son to you. Dick, you've got to quit this. . . ."

"It's not the same," DeFore insisted.

"The hell it's not the same. You figure blood makes that much difference? It doesn't, Dick, believe me, it doesn't." Ethan looked over at his son-in-law. He swallowed hard and his face turned pale. "Dick, you say us old-timers are good at keeping secrets. Well, let me tell you that a lot of youngsters are just as good at that. Dick, you look at me!"

Ethan's agitation as much as his quivering voice made not only Richard DeFore but also John stare at him. Both forgot everything else for the moment. Neither of them had ever seen Ethan MacCallister so worked up, so shaken and troubled as he was now.

"Dick," exclaimed Ethan in a low, savage tone, "you're forcing me to this, damn you! You're forcing me to prove to you I know what I'm talking about. You say it's not the same as if Travis was your own flesh and blood. Well, Ruth is not my real daughter."

Ethan stood there breathing painfully, his normally calm face twisted, his steady eyes misty. Behind him John made a little strangled gasp. DeFore stood dumbly staring, his jaw hanging slack.

"That's right," Ethan continued, rushing on, pushing his words all together to make them steady. "Ruth was six months old when I married her mother. Her pa was killed in the war. She's not my own child . . . my own flesh and blood. Now, damn you, DeFore, tell me it's not the same, and I'll tell you you're just plain wrong. I raised that girl. She's been more daughter to me than maybe my own child could have been."

"Ethan," John said, his voice almost a whisper. "Does Ruth know this?"

Ethan whipped around. "Of course she knows it. What kind of a man do you think I am, that I'd not tell a girl she had a father who died fighting to preserve his country?"

"She . . . she never said a thing about it to me, Ethan."

"Why should she? *I* raised her. *I'm* the only father she's ever known."

Ethan caught himself, forced himself to stop, to stand a long moment without saying anything more, to bring his tumultuous emotions under control. Then he said: "You think only the old-timers have secrets, Dick? You think you're the only one with a hurt in his heart? I'd have given a lot if Ruth had been my own flesh and blood . . . the first ten years of her life . . . but after that I knew something you're too blind to see. She *was* my daughter and she always will be. The same applies to Travis and you . . . if you'd just quit living in the past long enough to take a good long look at the present, of which you're a part, Dick DeFore, whether you like it or not."

Ethan turned, flung up his reins, and put his foot in the stirrup.

DeFore came out of his shock and said: "Where you going? What are you figuring on doing?"

"Get that damned gunfighter, that's what I came up here for . . . ," Ethan said, then paused to get his breathing back under control. "Well, that's part of what I came up here for anyway."

"Ethan," DeFore said, "wait a minute. What other thing did you come up here for?"

"To save an old fool from himself, I reckon," Ethan replied, and turned his horse. "Come along, John. I got to get down off this mesa."

But DeFore intervened. He stepped up, caught Ethan's reins at the bit, saying: "Wait, my horse is around back. I'd like to ride along with you."

Ethan looked down flintily. "Take your hand off those reins. You ride anywhere you want to up here, it's your land, but I'll be damned if you ride with me."

DeFore dropped his hand, shifted back one step, and gazed steadily upward until Ethan turned his mount and started back across the little plateau toward that downward trail. John rode along behind him.

Neither of them spoke until, a half hour later, they were down again into the broken country west of the stage road. Then Ethan drew rein, got down, went over, and sat upon a big boulder without looking at John. He ran a pained gaze toward the south where the town of Winchester lay invisible under a blanket of dusk.

For a long while John left him alone. He had a smoke. He examined both their animals. He walked out where he could see the faintly lighted peaks around them. He sought movement at those places, some sign that DeFore's riders were scanning the darkening land, or that Thorne's men were stealthily approaching.

He was still standing like this when from behind him, Ethan said: "See anything?" His voice was almost normal again.

"No, nothing," John answered, and walked back to squat down beside Ethan. "You were dead right up there," he told his father-in-law. "Dead right. But it hurt to say all that, didn't it, Ethan?"

"It hurt, son. You're damned right it hurt. That's the first time since Ruth's mother and I came to this country I ever told a living soul that story."

"Ethan, I got to say something. I just hope to hell I'm half the man you are . . . someday."

Ethan took out a bandanna, blew his nose thunderously, and stuffed the bandanna back in his pocket. His voice turning brisk again, he said: "You got any more tobacco, son? I'm about out and right now I sure need a smoke."

John handed over the makings.

Once he had built and lit a cigarette, Ethan

leaned back and watched the westward sky flame out, watched little streamers of night step delicately down along the far-away ridges. For a long time he was quiet. Finally though, he seemed to bring himself back to the present, for he said: "You know, nothing's going to happen up here in the dark. Why don't we head back for town?"

"You reckon we should?"

Ethan stood up. "Yeah," he muttered, and swung astride his horse.

They rode in a southerly direction until they could make out the stage road, then took that, still walking their horses along, each silent, each thoughtful and pensive. They were almost to the drop-off leading down out of Cheyenne Pass when two gunshots sounded clearly back where they had been.

Ethan whipped around. "Wrong! We're not going back!" he barked. "Come on!"

They went back swiftly toward the center of the pass, showing no mercy to their horses.

CHAPTER FIFTEEN

There were some lingering last vestiges of dusk upon the peaks and part way down the farthest slopes, but none of this provided any worthwhile degree of lightness to the pass itself, and there would be no moon this night, only feeble starshine that only faintly brightened the hostile atmosphere.

MacCallister rode along until he heard another gunshot, then he halted, sat his horse a moment, plumbing the onward gloom and trying to place the location of those shooters.

Klinger gestured toward the east and said: "Off there somewhere, I think."

All Ethan said in response was: "Watch for muzzle blast."

But it wasn't the crimson flash of a gunshot that finally moved them, it was the keening cry of a man.

"This way," muttered Ethan, and led off easterly back into that broken country they had so recently left. He rode slowly, not hurrying, attempting to make as little noise as possible. The night was full of peril, not only from Thorne's men but also from DeFore's riders, who would shoot at moving targets first and investigate later.

They dismounted where a butte to the west

shielded them and stopped the paleness coming down from that direction. They tied their horses and moved out, Winchesters in hand. But no more firing erupted, not for a long while, which left them lost as to which way to go.

MacCallister halted beside a twisted oak tree, listened, then lifted his shoulders and dropped them. "Don't know," he murmured. "DeFore sent his men to scatter out. We could get shot by walking out in front of one of them."

"You reckon the others are Thorne's crew?"

"Got to be, John, got to be. Who else would come charging up here for a battle?"

A sudden gunshot exploded a hundred yards ahead and slightly to the left. John would have moved out, but Ethan threw up an arm detaining him.

Ethan stood rigidly and stared. A second shot erupted, this one farther south than the first one and they both caught the flash of that blast. Whoever fired that second shot had been aiming straight where the first shot had blasted out.

Ethan put his head back and whispered: "Can't tell which is which, but one of 'em is Thorne's man. That fellow to the south is closest, so let's take him."

They started forward, Ethan in the lead, John following. They were careful not to make a sound. Between where they'd left the horses and the place where that second gunshot had come from was perhaps a thousand yards, all of it around the conical base of an up-ended granite spire. When he came across loose gravel underfoot, Ethan halted, listened, then angled to the west to get clear of the shale rock. This required time. It was also dangerous because the moment they left the solid darkness of that spire, they were out of reach of its protection.

For three hundred feet they went westward, then the grass firmed up underfoot. Ethan traveled in a half-circling way back to the northeast. He hadn't gone far when some big, tumbled boulders showed dead gray against the skyline. He set his course for this protection. When he had just about reached the big rocks, a furious flurry of gunshots broke out farther north. This seemed to trigger the raw nerves of every unseen fighter in the pass. At once a fusillade of shots erupted, red flames flashed against the dark night, gun thunder shattered the hush, and caroming echoes bounced off buttes and peaks and rolled flat out down the long cañons.

Ethan and his son-in-law moved quickly in among the boulders and crouched there, waiting out this storm.

John leaned his head over to say to Ethan: "This is senseless. How can any of them hope to accomplish anything in the dark?"

Ethan thought a moment, then replied: "I think Thorne figured on catching DeFore and his crew all bunched up. He probably figured to make one smashing attack . . . get the old man, scatter his riders, and have it all finished before night came fully down."

"Well, he sure missed the mark if that's what he had in mind," John said.

"Yeah. But Thorne didn't know the old man wouldn't fight all bunched up. He'd have no idea DeFore would scatter his riders around the peaks, each man to fight independently, because, you see, Thorne was figuring on fighting like soldiers do, and he tackled the wrong man for that. DeFore's an old-timer. He's fought in these hills before. He knows the best way to wage warfare in country like this is the same way the Indians used to do it . . . each man for himself, then, if an enemy overruns one position, all he gets is one man because the others shift around and hit him again and again."

John continued to crouch there as he listened. He was thinking about this strategy Ethan had just explained as much as he was listening to the dwindling gunfire. When that swift exchange eventually died, he said: "I keep getting more and more respect for that old devil, Ethan."

The former sheriff said nothing. He stood up cautiously, peered around, tapped John's arm, and headed off eastward, moving craftily from boulder to boulder until a gun erupted no more than a hundred feet ahead. Quickly, he stepped behind a rock, carefully leaned his carbine there, removed his spurs, his hat, and his shell belt, took only his pistol and got flat down to peer carefully around the base of the rock.

John also removed his spurs and put aside his Winchester, but he kept on his hat and shell belt as he eased down close to his father-in-law. He whispered: "Give me cover in case I make a noise crawling up there and he fires back here."

Ethan put out a restraining hand and shook his head. "I'll do it," he said vehemently. "I'm a single man." He eased out and began crawling. John had his lips parted to protest, but Ethan was already crawling rapidly, swinging his hips and his shoulders. John could see this was something his father-in-law had done many times before. Then Ethan was swallowed up by the dark.

For fifty feet Ethan had no trouble since there were big old thunderhead boulders around for him to keep between himself and whoever that gunman was up ahead, but the second fifty feet was open and covered with sharp-edged small, gravelly stones. It was this second fifty feet that mattered.

Ethan jumped back and forth as he advanced, but he was compelled to halt where the man-sized rocks gave way to that open space. Here, he selected a vantage point that offered good sighting ahead, toward the rocks where that invisible gunman was hiding. He drew his six-gun, made a solid arm rest, lay the gun across it, half balancing upon solid granite, and waited. If the gunman up there heard Ethan coming, raised up, and twisted around, Ethan would have him. But it didn't happen like that at all, and when the time finally came Ethan did not dare fire.

Ethan crawled out upon the exposed, stony clearing, halting from time to time, and crawled along when he was satisfied it was safe to do so. He was praying for another of those unreasoning bursts of wild gunfire, but none came. He almost reached the boulder behind which the unseen gunman was crouching when, off to his right somewhere, but also in the rocks, a man's quick, startled shout rang out one second ahead of a blasting gunshot.

Dust and stones exploded two feet off, showering Ethan. There was another gunman in the boulders now, evidently recently arrived and trying to make his way over where the first gunman was hiding. This man had sighted Ethan creeping down upon his friend, had cried his warning, and almost simultaneously fired at Ethan.

John was aghast. From back where he stood, it seemed that Ethan had been struck, but he wasted only a second on that possibility. He whirled, slammed a shot in the direction of this second gunman, and effectively drove Ethan's attacker to cover.

But on ahead the damage had been done. Whether the first gunman thought that shot had been fired by friend or foe made no difference. One thing that gunman was positive of—there was lethal danger somewhere behind him.

Ethan, anticipating this reaction, lunged ahead the final fifteen feet, got in close to the rock behind which this man lay hidden, pressed flat there, and waited, scarcely breathing. Behind him, John fired again. This time the bullet struck unyielding stone and made a chilling noise as it changed its course and went upward in the night.

This firing, though, finally accomplished what Ethan had wished earlier might happen, but which he certainly did not care about happening now as he lay exposed behind that rough-faced stone. It prompted other nervous men in the roundabout night to open up again, firing quite blindly, for the most part.

For what seemed an eternity the man on the opposite side of Ethan's rock did not fire at all, nor did he make any kind of a sound which would have told Ethan where he was, exactly, and what he was doing. But as that second wild fusillade died away, Ethan caught the scrape of metal—maybe a belt buckle—over shale. His enemy was inching around the big stone to look out toward the rear. Ethan pushed his six-gun forward toward the rounding base of the same stone, and scarcely breathed.

Once more John got off a shot. He was very effectively neutralizing the other hidden gunman. Then silence settled, drew out to its absolute maximum.

Just as Ethan could feel his muscles instinctively bunching from remaining in one position so long, a softly sibilant little abrasive sound came from beyond the rock. This told Ethan that his adversary was coming around the south end of the boulder, the direction Ethan was facing.

He raised his six-gun, placed his thumb pad down hard over the hammer, and held his breath.

The man crawled a few inches more, then he became still for so long Ethan was thinking he had stopped and picked a new position. But he hadn't, for he could see a good deal of the little clearing and was taking time to study it. Then the man continued on again, less carefully now, as though upon finding that expanse to the rear empty, he was encouraged to feel safe.

Ethan caught sight of a gun barrel first as his adversary pushcd his gun hand forward. The former sheriff kept his eyes trained on that length of blue steel. It stopped moving briefly, then came on again. All around was a great silence. It was as though Ethan and the unseen man were the only two people for miles around. The gun edged forward again, both barrel and cylinder were now in sight. Ethan raised his own weapon slightly, tightened his grip, and waited.

The man's fisted hand and wrist came into sight and Ethan threw all his weight into a savage downward chop. He felt his six-gun barrel strike solidly. The shock of that impact travelled all the way to Ethan's shoulder. He felt gristle and bone give way under the savage blow of his gun barrel striking that exposed wrist. Then the still unseen man gave a tremendous bound upward and let off a nerve-searing scream as he rolled out into sight. He grabbed for that smashed wrist with his good hand, and even when he saw Ethan rise up to crouch above him, his .45 less than five feet away, the injured cowboy continued to writhe.

The effect of that agonized scream seemed to have its instant effect elsewhere; men cried out at one another and threw shots wherever they had seen, or thought they had seen, movement.

Klinger fired again, but it was beginning to appear that his particular adversary had departed, evidently believing he'd stumbled into the midst of the opposition. At least John got back no return fire.

While this flashing bedlam ran on, Ethan retrieved the injured man's weapon, pushed it into his waistband, and motioned for his prisoner to get up. He did not know this man. Earlier, he had thought he might be one of those hardcases he and John had ordered out of Winchester, but he was not. He was a perfect stranger to Ethan. When he staggered upright, Ethan prodded him along with his .45, herding his prisoner back toward the boulder where John was waiting. When John stepped out to lend a hand, Ethan kept on going. The three of them got back where the carbines were and here, finally, Ethan sat down, dropped his hat upon the back of his head, buckled on his spurs, holstered his six-gun, and retrieved his Winchester. Not until then did he make a slow study of his prisoner.

The unknown cowboy was moaning behind gritted teeth and wagging his head with pain from his shattered wrist. He seemed oblivious to MacCallister and Klinger. For a time they paid their captive slight heed as they remained alert for any movement or sound. The night beyond this place was as silent and still as it had been before the fight started.

"Pulled out, I reckon," Ethan mused, squaring back around to regard the cowboy. "I think our friend's scream did that for us. About all it takes in the night to scatter brave men is a scream like that."

MacCallister stepped over, considered the man's right arm, yanked off his neckerchief, then held out his hand for John's neckerchief. Wordlessly and efficiently, he began bandaging the unresisting man's shattered wrist. He finished up by making a sling out of the stranger's belt and neckerchief. It was crude but it was adequate, and with the first pain gradually subsiding, the strange rider looked at his captors—looked longest at the badges they both wore.

"What's your name?" John asked the man.

"Carl Nolte."

"Where's Ray Thorne, Carl?"

"I don't know. I don't know where anyone is. This was crazy, tryin' to get that old man in the night when he had his crew and the law up here with him."

"Did you know the law was up here with him, Carl?"

"Hell no! If I had I wouldn't have gotten into this thing."

"But you knew the law was after you fellows and Thorne."

The cowboy shook his head emphatically. "I knew no such a thing," he said. "Thorne told us the law favored the stage line, but that it couldn't get involved, so the stage line had to force the pass open by itself."

John looked at Ethan. Obviously John was skeptical of Nolte's statement.

All Ethan said was: "Come on, let's find DeFore and get out of this place. This fellow needs a doctor and we need some supper."

They took their prisoner back over the same ground they had traversed getting to this spot, and ultimately got safely back to their horses. There was not a sound anywhere in the night.

With their animals untied and in hand, Ethan

raised his voice in a shout: "DeFore? This is Ethan MacCallister. Are you all right?"

For a long moment no reply came back, then DeFore's rough voice called back profanely, saying he was fine, but that he didn't think the stage company hirelings were.

To this, Ethan called back: "Meet at your place, DeFore. Pull out when you think it's safe. We've got an injured prisoner, so we're pulling out now."

"It's safe right now," came back DeFore's growling voice. "They've pulled out, I heard 'em go."

"Which way?"

"West, damn 'em . . . off into the badlands west of here."

Ethan turned on the prisoner. "That sound right?" he asked.

"It's right," mumbled the captive. "The plan was to hit fast, get the old man, and keep right on goin' west into the hills where no pursuit could overtake us."

John mounted, kicked out his booted left foot, and thrust a hand downward toward Nolte. Without a word the prisoner grasped that hand, used the left stirrup, and sprang up to settle behind John's cantle.

Ethan let those two ride on ahead twenty or thirty feet, then he mounted his horse and moved out easterly toward the stage road, and on across it to the run of tilted land which led down through dingy cañons to DeFore's home ranch.

Nothing was said the full length of that trip. Each man was absorbed by his own grim thoughts.

CHAPTER SIXTEEN

It was well past midnight before DeFore and his riders came walking their horses on into the yard. One of them had a bullet hole through the fleshy part of his upper leg and while this did not, upon examination by lantern, turn out to be serious, to his chiding companions the injured man blisteringly suggested that if they didn't think his wound was much, they should try riding a horse over rough ground in the dark with a wound just like it.

DeFore left one of his men to care for this indignant rider, brought the remaining two with him to the porch of his ranch house where MacCallister, Klinger, and their prisoner were waiting. He unlocked his front door and stamped in, mumbling a terse invitation for the others to come inside.

As soon as some lamps had been lighted DeFore stepped up and glared at the prisoner. He didn't say anything. He didn't have to, his look was venomous enough to compensate for anything he could have said. He sent one of his riders to awaken his cook and have some food prepared, then he walked over and stopped, wide-legged, in front of Ethan. As he'd done with the prisoner, DeFore stood and looked but said nothing for a long while. Finally, he pushed out his hand.

"Shake, Ethan. I'm plumb sorry I put you in that spot up at the chapel. I had no idea how it was with Ruthie."

Ethan made no move to take the older man's hand nor did he follow out this line of talk. Instead, he said: "As soon as we've eaten we'll take the prisoner down to town. As for Thorne and the others . . ."

"Ethan, forget Thorne and the others. They aren't important now."

"What do you mean . . . not important? It was their intention to kill you, DeFore, and kill the rest of us right along with you if we interfered."

"Ethan, listen to me," DeFore said, beginning to look exasperated at MacCallister's chilly attitude. "Listen to me for a minute."

"All right, I'm listening."

"Shake," DeFore prodded, again extending his hand.

"You go to the devil, Dick DeFore. You've always had some idea you were rough and tough and aloof. Well, go on being that way for all I care."

"Dammit all, Ethan, I didn't understand before. I swear to you I didn't."

"Leave my daughter out of it."

"I'm not talking about your daughter, confound it. I'm talking about what you said up there by the chapel. About me living too much in the past

188

and not in the present." DeFore paused, squinted up his eyes, and extended his hand once again. "All I'm trying to say now is that I been wrong . . . that you did me a favor up there on the butte and I appreciate it. Now will you shake?"

Ethan was standing stiffly and unrelentingly hostile. He looked with a fierce coldness at DeFore. Beside him his son-in-law faintly sighed, bringing Ethan's head around. John was looking straight at him, and there was the faintest hint of disillusionment in John's gaze. Ethan saw this. He also understood it. So he reached out, grasped DeFore's hand, pumped it once, hard, and dropped it. Then he turned away saying shortly: "All right, now let's get on with what's got to be done."

DeFore turned. To his riders he said: "Saddle us some fresh horses. We'll hit the trail of this confounded two-gun man, and this time we'll keep riding until we get him. But first we grub."

The cowboys left the house just as a tousle-headed, wizened, and crippled man poked a head through a partially opened doorway and said garrulously: "Come and get it! And if it ain't enough that's just too danged bad, but at two in the consarned mornin' it's all you're goin' to get!"

DeFore led the way to the house kitchen. The tousle-headed man was nowhere in evidence.

"My cook," explained DeFore, looking apologetic. "He's one of the first riders I ever had and . . . well, he's sort of independent sometimes."

They sat at the table, the four of them, and when Ethan poured coffee for their one-handed prisoner, Nolte said: "You fellows know somethin'? I think the whole blessed bunch of you are plumb crazy, fightin' over that lousy road up there in the rocks."

DeFore flared at this, saying: "Who asked you what you thought, you lousy two-bit drifter? What do you mean, taking Thorne's money to bushwhack me?"

"Mister," snapped back Nolte, "I never bushwhacked anyone in my life, not even a cranky old maverick like you. All I did was agree to come up here and help Thorne in what I thought was a legitimate fight. So did my pardner. But after listenin' to all the talk that's been goin' on lately, I keep wonderin' just what all this is really about."

Klinger calmly told the captive about DeFore's insistence that travelers, especially stagecoach travelers, stop tracking over his land. John did not say why DeFore insisted on this and the cowboy never asked.

All he said was: "Shucks, and that's what this battle is about?"

"No," said Ethan. "There's more. Thorne's trying to make a battle out of it so he'll keep drawing gunfighter wages from the stage company."

"Well," said the youthful cowboy in that same dryly disgusted tone of voice, "why don't you simpletons fix it so's there won't be no cause for a fight?"

DeFore reddened at both the insult and the condescending sound of the rider's voice, but when he would have verbally lashed out, Ethan stopped him with an upraised hand.

"How?" he asked the injured man.

The cowboy took a long drink of coffee, set the cup aside, and said: "Mister DeFore wants the stages to quit lettin' their passengers out up in the pass while the horses are blown, is that it?"

"It is," snapped DeFore.

"Then," Nolte said, his eyes traveling to the others around the table, "downgrade a quarter mile below the top out, have a crew flatten out a place beside the road . . . a turnout . . . where drivers can turn off and stop to blow the horses. No one's goin' to get out of the coaches down there where there's nothin' but brush and rocks, and maybe rattlesnakes, too, so the horses get their rest, then the coaches push on up into the pass and keep right on goin' because, with rested teams, they'll have no reason to stop."

When Carl Nolte stopped speaking, Ethan looked at John, then on over at DeFore. None of them said anything for a long while. This solution was so simple, should have been so obvious, and was so easy to achieve, that it had not up until now occurred to a single one of them.

DeFore cleared his throat, picked up the platter of fried meat, and held it out to the cowboy. "Have some more steak," he said. "Here, let me cut it for you, boy."

Ethan forked in more food and masticated thoughtfully. Eventually, he put aside his utensils and said: "It's Thorne's fault, damn him. He's kept us all so on edge and keyed up we never had time to think of that. Dick?"

"Yeah."

"Come down to town and talk to that stage company fellow we've got locked up at the jailhouse."

"What for?"

"Tell him how much you want to turn Cheyenne Pass into a dedicated roadway. He's got the power to say yes. He told John and me he had a blank check for expenses up here."

DeFore finished cutting Nolte's meat, sat back a moment, then said: "Hell, Ethan, I don't want their lousy money. All I ever wanted was for folks to respect my rights."

"Then," Klinger said, speaking up for the first time, "dedicate the damned road. Give it to the county. Give a strip the width of the road, Mister DeFore, and keep everything on both sides. Post it. Put up no trespassing signs. Have the stage line agree to construct the turnout and not to stop anywhere else in the pass."

DeFore listened to all this. So did Ethan. The two older men gazed steadily at one another for a moment after John had stopped speaking.

DeFore gently inclined his head. "Done," he said. "That's exactly what I'll do." He furrowed his brow at Ethan. "You think the stage company will go along with that?"

"If they don't," Ethan said, "I promise you one thing, Dick. They'll sure wish they had before I'm through with 'em. And as for the trespassing, just leave that to John and me. After we've arrested one or two trespassers, I got a notion folks will wake up soon enough to understand they had better obey your signs."

The injured cowboy finished eating, pushed back his plate, looked around, wagging his head. "You fellows sure aren't very bright," he stated. "Havin' a war over somethin' as ridiculous as this crooked old dirt roadway."

Ethan put a skeptical gaze around. "No, we weren't," he said with deceptive mildness. "But on the other hand, young fellow, you don't see any of us with busted arms, either, because we were gullible enough to let a gunfighter like Ray Thorne talk us into getting on the wrong side of the law."

Nolte looked over at Ethan with an expression which became gradually worried. "Didn't think of it before," he said quietly, as though testing the idea now, "but, by golly, I reckon I am an outlaw, ain't I?"

DeFore got up, kicked aside his chair, and said: "Ethan, how about it? The boy did us a favor."

Klinger stood up, too. So did the cowboy. The last man up from the table was MacCallister, and he didn't immediately reply to DeFore's question. He borrowed John's makings again, emptied what remained of the tobacco into a troughed paper, folded the thing carefully, wet it, and sealed it. He stuck the cigarette between his lips, struck a match, and as he lit up, he gazed with narrowed eyes over at the cowboy. "Too bad you've got a busted wing," he stated.

"What of that?" demanded the prisoner.

"Well, if you were sound, I'd let you maybe work out of this mess by building that turnout yourself."

The youth snorted. "Deputy, I can work as well with one hand as most fellows can work with two. You give me one helper, two shovels and two picks, and I'll build the dog-goned turnout."

DeFore grinned. He was a hard man himself, and like all hard men, he liked toughness in others.

"Go you one better," he said, addressing both lawmen. "You two let me supervise the building of that turnout, and, when it's finished, I'll put this young buck on as a permanent ranch rider."

194

DeFore didn't wait for them to agree or disagree. He turned his tough smile upon the cowboy, saying: "Well, what about it? You're a drifter, aren't you?"

"Yes, sir."

"And you need work?"

"Yes, sir."

"Well, you want a riding job on my ranch or don't you?"

"Yes, sir, I'd sure like that. I like this country, and, with some few exceptions, I like the folks in it."

"John," said Ethan, "you're the sheriff."

"To tell you the truth, Ethan," Klinger said, "I never really figured on locking this one up . . . not after he explained how he happened to be riding with Thorne."

"Then that's settled," boomed big Richard DeFore. "Come on, let's get our horses and head for Winchester. This boy needs a doctor to properly set that arm, and after that I figure you lawmen ought to be willing to do a little more riding . . . at least until we run down this two-gun tinhorn and settle his hash for him one way or another."

They exited the house, found their animals at the outside rack along with three of DeFore's remaining men, and they all swung up simultaneously, whirled the horses, and struck out southward down through the gloomy cañons.

DeFore's riders went on ahead. The old cowman rode stirrup with Ethan MacCallister, and the last two in this cavalcade were John Klinger and the cowboy named Carl Nolte.

There was a little speculation about where Thorne and his remaining men might be, but after Nolte told the others he knew only that they meant to camp in the hills to the west for the balance of the night, there wasn't much need for more speculation on that subject.

This did not, however, mean that the resolve of these men had lessened one bit. It hadn't, but other things had arisen now to fill their thoughts solemnly as they passed downcountry toward a slumbering Winchester.

When they were still a half mile out, off in the east a pale brightness began to softly glow. Dawn was not very far off now.

Chapter Seventeen

The lot of them left their horses at the livery barn. DeFore and his men walked down to the jailhouse to see Travis Browne, and Ethan, along with his son-in-law, took Carl Nolte over to Dr. Shirley's home, banged loudly and relentlessly on the door until the sleepy-eyed physician opened it, and ushered them in.

The doctor looked dubiously at Ethan, at John, then he wordlessly led the three men into his dispensary where he examined the broken, swelling wrist and disapprovingly shook his head.

"Cowboy, I can't do a thing for that arm until the swelling has subsided. Why didn't you come to me the moment it happened?"

Nolte made a crooked smile. "Sure meant to," he drawled, "but things kept interferin'."

"Well, I'll fix you up with a bowl and some ice water. You can soak the hand and wrist in that until some of the swelling goes down, then perhaps we can set the thing."

John nodded at Nolte and turned to leave. So did Ethan, but before leaving the dispensary he said: "Carl, you're on the right side now. Stay on it."

The doctor turned away. Nolte looked around

at Ethan and John. "You don't have to wait," he said. "I won't run out. Go ahead and look for Thorne."

Outside again, Klinger and MacCallister started southward. There were two lighted windows on their side of the roadway. One was near the lower end of town at the jailhouse, the other was mid-way between, at Hank Weaver's office.

As they paced along in the cool dawn, John said: "What the devil would get Hank up so early?"

Instead of replying, Ethan swung over when they came abreast of the office door and pushed on inside.

Weaver was behind his counter busy with his clipboard and a sheaf of loose papers. He looked surprised to see the sheriff and deputy and his eyelids twitched as he stared at the two.

"Up kind of early, aren't you?" asked John.

"Got a southbound coach to send out this morning," Weaver said, his eyes back on the papers he was shuffling.

"How come?"

"Them mine fellows you two walked out on yesterday . . . they're bringing in the bullion." Weaver looked up and shook his head at the lawmen. "That sure wasn't very mannerly, what you fellows did yesterday when I brought those fellows down to talk to you."

"Well now, Hank," Ethan began in a soothing

198

tone, "we had something a heap more important on our minds then a social chat." Ethan nodded at Hank before he turned and started back for the door. John followed him and the pair were almost across the room when Weaver spoke again.

"Yeah I know, you were trying to stop old man DeFore from killing the company's special guard."

With one hand on the latch, Ethan turned back, frowning. "Special guard?" he repeated.

"Thorne. He told me last night how you fellows tried to keep DeFore from riding into town."

Klinger's eyes widened at this misinformation. He kept staring over at Weaver. But Ethan was surprised for barely a second before an idea struck him suddenly.

"Hank, when did you talk to Thorne?" the former sheriff asked.

"When? Why, last night. I just told you that."

"What time last night?"

Weaver made a face, thought a moment, then said: "About eleven o'clock, I'd say. Why?"

"No, Hank, I think it must have been closer to midnight."

"All right. Maybe it was. I know I was just finishing up around here when he rode in. He had three fellows with him. The two went on over to the hotel, but Thorne stopped by here and we got to talking. That's when he told me you . . ."

"Hank," John snapped, breaking through that

quiet run of Weaver's words. "What else did you two talk about . . . maybe this bullion coach?"

"Well, sure, I wanted him to guard it. To go along with his men as outriders, you see, because with just those two mine company men inside, that wasn't much protection for seventy thousand dollars' worth of gold."

"Seventy thousand dollars' worth of gold," whispered John, staring over at Weaver.

Weaver bobbed his head up and down.

John would have said more, but Ethan suddenly lay a hand upon his son-in-law's arm to silence him. "Hank," Ethan said, "what time is this bullion coach pulling out this morning?"

"An hour from now. But if we keep standing around here talking, it'll never get ready."

"Clem Whipple going to drive?"

"Yes, and one of the mine guards will be up on the box with Clem while the other one is inside with the bullion."

"And Thorne will be on hand to outride. Is that right?"

"Well, not exactly, Ethan. That's what I wanted him to do, but he said it'd be better if him and his men met the coach south of town, maybe down by the pass, and escorted it from there. He said it'd be a dead giveaway if folks saw him and his riders escorting the coach from town."

"Oh, sure," Ethan said. "Sure, Hank, it'd be a dead giveaway." He paused long enough to cast an ironic look at John, then he added: "If Thorne is going to meet the coach at the southward pass, he'll have left town by now, I reckon."

"Sure," agreed Weaver. "He'd have to have left at least an hour back. Maybe two hours ago."

"Thanks," Ethan said as he opened the door and passed through. As John turned to leave with Ethan, Weaver called out: "Any time, fellows. Any time at all."

Before John could say a word, Ethan turned around and said: "Go check the livery barn. Find out what time they left and how many men were with Thorne. I'll be down at the jailhouse. Hurry, son."

John hurried back northward while Ethan went just as swiftly down where DeFore and his men were waiting in the jailhouse. As Ethan burst into the office, DeFore, over at the little woodstove swishing lukewarm coffee in a crockery mug, looked up and said: "Sure took you fellows a long time to rout one doctor out of bed."

MacCallister stepped over to the desk, perched upon the edge of it, and told DeFore and his crew: "Thorne rode back here last night after the fight up at Cheyenne Pass."

DeFore and his men stared at the former sheriff, saying nothing for a long while. Finally, DeFore set aside his crockery cup. "Here?" he said. "Is he still here now?"

"No. There's a bullion coach heading out of

town within an hour. Thorne knows about it. He and his riders are going to meet that coach down at South Pass . . . as escorts for the stage company."

"What!" roared DeFore. "Are you being funny, Ethan?"

"Yeah, I'm being funny . . . about as funny as a poke in the eye with a sharp stick. Now listen to me, you fellows. When John returns, you're going to be deputized, then we're going along behind that coach."

"Behind it," growled DeFore. "Ethan, it'll be sunup in another hour. Thorne, if he's on ahead, will see us on the road and we'll never get close enough to . . ."

"Dick, will you shut up and listen?" Ethan snapped. "No, he's not going to see us, because we're not going to stay on the road after we leave town. I know that country down there like I know the back of my hand. We'll cut eastward and come out in the broken country down there. At all times we'll keep the hills between us where Thorne figures to rob the coach."

"If we ride out and around," stated one of the DeFore riders, "we'll lose time, Deputy."

Ethan shook his head. "Clem Whipple's going to be on the box of that coach. I'll see to it that Clem takes plenty of time."

Ethan picked up a ring of keys from the desk, tossed them to Dick DeFore, and nodded toward the cell-block door. "Go see Travis if you like," he said, and as the DeFore men moved over toward that oaken panel, Klinger entered from the softly lighted outside roadway. He shot a look over where DeFore's men were passing beyond sight into the cell-block, then swung toward his father-in-law.

"About two hours ago, Thorne got a fresh horse for himself and so did the three men with him," John announced. "The nighthawk at the barn said he recognized two of those fellows as the hardcases you and I ordered out of town."

"Thorne happen to say anything to the nighthawk?" Ethan asked.

"Nothing at all. Just hired the critters, paid in advance for them, left four jaded horses, and rode right on out."

"I been doing some thinking, John," Ethan said. "I'll go talk to Clem about taking his time so as not to get too far ahead of us. That'll take care of the hold-up." He glanced at DeFore. "There's still this other thing about you, Dick, and Cheyenne Pass, and Mather back there in the cell and his dog-goned stage company. When you go back to see Travis, don't say anything."

"Go on, Ethan," John urged. "I'll make sure there's no trouble at this end."

"Better yet, while I'm up talking to Clem, get Mather out of jail, give him back his little pistol, and take him up to the stage office. Then I want you to make sure that he's on that southbound coach."

John's face brightened with understanding. He made a slow, soft smile. "Sure," he assented, "I'll do that. If talking won't convince Mister Mather his company made a bad mistake in hiring Thorne, maybe being smack dab in the middle of a hold-up down at South Pass, will convince him."

"Exactly," agreed Ethan. "So you better get back there and make sure he doesn't know in advance what's going on. We know he's going to buck like a bay steer about being put on the coach and sent out of Winchester. Just be damned sure he's aboard when Clem pulls out. After that, meet me at the livery barn. Any questions?"

When John shook his head, Ethan stood, stretched, eyed that cheerily bubbling coffee pot over on the stove, and shook his head. He then winked at his son-in-law, and walked out of the office.

Winchester was beginning to stir, to show signs of life along its main thoroughfare. Here and there merchants were unlocking their stores, setting out sidewalk displays, calling back and forth to one another as they prepared for another pleasant day. Up at the stage office a coach was drawn in beside the plank walk, its six fresh horses

204

standing impatiently, facing southward, and a little knot of men were stationed on the walk beside it. Two of them Ethan recognized as the mine company men, along with Clem Whipple and Hank Weaver. The fifth man was a hostler from the back lot, and he was more concerned with checking tugs and harness, singletrees and doubletrees, than with the cryptic conversation going on among the others.

MacCallister nodded pleasantly at the men as he came up. He nodded and caught Clem's arm and drew him off to one side. Weaver and the mine company men nodded back, but then ignored Ethan and Clem as they considered the papers Weaver was holding out to them. Their brief, guarded sentences were barely distinguishable over where Ethan swiftly sketched in the situation to Clem.

The longer he listened, the wider Clem's eyes became. Finally, when Ethan was finished, he said quietly: "Holy hell, Ethan . . . Thorne's going to hold us up? The minute I laid eyes on him I figured he was trouble four ways from the middle, but I never figured him for a common highwayman."

Ethan said: "Do you have any idea how much gold is on your stage today?"

"Well, not exactly. But maybe about . . ."

"Seventy thousand dollars' worth!" Ethan informed him.

Clem gasped and swallowed, staring at the deputy.

"Now the difference between a gunfighter like Ray Thorne and a highwayman, is just about that much money. In fact, for seventy thousand, I think half the tinhorns in Sherman County would take a chance on trying to perpetrate a robbery."

The stage driver closed his mouth, thought a moment, then vigorously bobbed his head up and down. "I'll do like you say, Ethan. I'll kill time so's you boys will be sure and get into position before I hit South Pass. But for gosh sakes, don't fail to be there. I got a wife and kid, you know, and sitting up there on the box, I'm a perfect target."

Ethan put a hand upon Whipple's shoulder. "We'll be in position, Clem. Don't you worry about that. But if things get too hot, turn that coach around, and head back before you're down into the pass. And one more thing . . . you'll have Charles Mather aboard. He's the bigwig from the Denver office. If he starts shouting orders at you, just remember this . . . in Sherman County, he's just another passenger as far as the law's concerned. You do what I've told you, and never mind Mather."

"Sure, Ethan." The stage driver shifted his footing, looked worriedly around and back again. "Anyone else know about this? I mean, do those mine guards have any idea . . . ?"

"No. You'll be the only man on that stage who knows. I think it best to keep it this way too. Don't you?"

Clem's worried look kept deepening. "I guess so," he eventually muttered. "Just don't fail us, Ethan."

"We won't. I promise you. Now go on back and act like nothing is going to happen."

Shakily, Clem said: "You know any way to act brave when you're scairt to death?"

Ethan did not reply to this, instead he walked on toward the livery barn, leaving Clem and those others making their final preparations at coach side.

The livery man was just heading inside when Ethan came along. He had just finished breakfast and was sucking on a toothpick. He halted as Ethan came up, smiled, commenting: "Going to be another pretty day. I sure enjoy this time of year . . . warm and peaceful and not too hot."

MacCallister nodded agreeably. "You never can tell how hot things will get, Lemuel," he stated as he walked inside and asked for two fresh horses.

Lemuel spat out his toothpick and nodded. As he headed to the stalls, he said to MacCallister: "Seen anything of that danged two-gun man lately, Ethan? There was a rumor going around town last night that he hired some drifters and was going to force a passage up through Cheyenne Pass."

Ethan examined the horses as the hostler brought them over for saddling when he answered, saying: "You never can tell about those gunfighters. Sometimes they only do what they're paid to do. Other times they get to thinking for themselves, and when that happens, there's likely to be hell to pay."

"Yep," agreed Sinclair. "That's sure the truth, Ethan."

CHAPTER EIGHTEEN

The stage pulled out just as the sun was beginning to show itself over the peaks to the east. Ten minutes later MacCallister and Klinger, riding on either side of DeFore, along with three of the rancher's men, left Winchester, heading southward. Neither the stage nor those six horsemen farther back seemed in any particular hurry.

As they cleared the south end of town, DeFore leaned out of his saddle to speak to Ethan. "Travis was fit to be tied that he couldn't get out and come along. He even said he'd ride in the coach."

Hearing this, John made a short snort. "If you think Travis was mad, you should've heard Charles Mather. He swore he'd see the governor . . . have the militia called out . . . and come back to Winchester with an Army." John shook his head ruefully. "You know, for a fat man who dresses like a genuine city dude, Mather sure can cuss."

They rode along, looking whiskery, travel stained, and grim. Someone sighting them for the first time could easily have mistaken the lot of them for an outlaw gang.

They cut easterly a mile below town, followed MacCallister as he led them around through the tree-scattered country down where Winchester

Valley ran along toward its meeting with those hulking black southernmost bulwarks, and did not speak until Ethan halted well east of the road and sat his horse, studying the onward dark slopes, down by the pass.

Then DeFore said: "So far so good. But why not keep on going?"

"Waiting," responded Ethan. "Waiting to catch reflected light off metal down there. We can be sure Thorne's in the rocks, but we've got to know where."

The stage was going along at a fast walk, moving through its own dust. Elsewhere the land was utterly empty under a brightly dazzling sun. Klinger grunted, lifted an arm, and pointed straight toward the east side of the pass where ragged lava rock lay in tumbled disarray. "Watch," he said as he lowered his arm. "In front of the pass on the left."

They all watched while sitting screened from sight, eventually catching the momentary flash of sunlight off metal.

Ethan eased out, saying: "Well, I reckon that settles that."

They rode ahead for a long half hour, stopped once more to gauge their progress in relation to the same progress of the stage, then went on again. Ethan led them far out and around until, as they came in behind the eastward broken country which sloped down toward the pass, the sun was behind them.

He explained his reasoning as they moved along slowly. "You know, I never worried too much about fellows shooting at me if the sun was in their eyes."

Where he finally halted and stepped down, they could see the coach no more than a half mile from the pass. They left their horses tied in a cluster of brush and went ahead on foot, each man with his Winchester in hand.

It was a rough route through the lava rock. Stones that cut as sharply as any knife cut their boots, snagged their clothing, and scratched their arms and legs. It did nothing to improve tempers already worn thin from being up all night in the saddle and stomachs long empty.

At a point, MacCallister left them to scout on ahead. The pass's visible entrance was less than a thousand yards ahead when he did this. He had traveled less than half that distance when he found four tethered horses standing drowsily where sunlight warmed their sides and rumps. The carbine boots of those saddles were empty, which told a story.

Ethan hurried back, informed the others, and brought them up where Thorne and his men had left their animals. Here, DeFore's riders methodically stripped off the saddles and bridles, leaving Thorne's horses tied only by ropes. Then the six of them crept along until, hearing men's voices dead ahead within a hundred feet of the roadway, they halted again.

DeFore leaned in close to Ethan's ear and spoke in little more than a whisper: "We got to fan out in order to cut 'em off north and south like we've already done by getting between them and their horses."

But MacCallister shook his head at this. "Too risky," he said. "From now on they'll hear any noise we make."

Although DeFore didn't agree, he eased ahead a few more feet with the others, getting down into the rocks where they would wait. Klinger had the best view to the north, so he was constantly reporting the progress of the stage. No sooner had he told them the stage was less than a quarter mile away, a Thorne man rose up dead ahead, having also eyed the position of the coach.

His voice sounding both garrulous and suspicious, he said: "Ray, how come 'em to be poking along like that? I never seen a bullion stage acting like it wanted to be stopped before."

Thorne's unmistakable response was immediate and dismissive: "Who cares why they're poking along? All we care about is that it's going to make this a lot easier."

MacCallister and Klinger exchanged a look. Dick DeFore raised his carbine and focused in at the tumbled rocks where he believed Thorne was positioned.

The stage's creaking, rattling noises came distinctly to all those waiting men now. It was close to the pass and it was still coming along slowly. In gazing over at it, MacCallister saw how it listed badly to the right. He smiled to himself for he knew that the rotund Charles Mather was the cause of that tilting.

The deputy slowly straightened up. It was not his intention to wait for Thorne to halt the coach for the elemental reason that with a man like Ray Thorne, this would be too dangerous. Thorne was a gunman. He would fire first and look second, and Ethan distinctly recalled Clem Whipple's concern about being a target up there on his coach seat.

But before Ethan could call out, or even alert his companions, Thorne suddenly jumped out into the roadway and threw up a carbine.

"Stop this coach! And you inside there, get out!" he yelled.

Clem watched as Thorne and his men appeared by the road, creeping out from their hiding places. He quickly set back on his lines, his heart pounding and his mouth going dry.

At the same time John Klinger sprang up, his gun levelled as he cried out: "Thorne! Throw down that gun!"

What MacCallister had anticipated happened.

Although he was taken entirely by surprise, the two-gun man whipped around and fired. He didn't aim at anything except the direction of Klinger's voice, but even so his bullet struck the rock in front of John throwing jagged pieces of stone into the sheriff's face. At the impact, John staggered back and DeFore, evidently believing Thorne had scored, sprang up with a raging howl and fired point-blank at the nearest of Thorne's crew. His slug caught one flush in the chest. Taken totally off guard, the man flung up his arms and went over backward, dead before he hit the ground.

MacCallister dropped his carbine, drew his .45 in a blur of speed, and shot at Thorne. The two-gun man staggered, switched position, and levered off a shot that drove the deputy sheriff into a quick crouch.

Thorne's remaining men were evidently too surprised to delve immediately into action. They moved among the rocks, trying to locate the position of DeFore and his riders who were filling the pass with thunderous gunfire. One of them dropped his gun and raised both arms high over his head. The second man ran out into the road, whirled, and fired his carbine from the hip, levering and firing as fast as he could work the firing mechanism. This man and Ray Thorne stood fully exposed; their fierce fire drove the Winchester posse down and kept them down.

Clem was shouting at his horses as he fought

them into a big lunge, trying to turn his heavy vehicle around and head back toward town. Both the mine guards were firing at Thorne and his companion, but aiming accurately from the hurricane deck of the shifting and rocking coach was impossible.

MacCallister peered around the base of the rock that shielded him, caught Thorne in his sights, and fired. Again the two-gun man staggered, but this time he also sagged.

DeFore's raging, bull-bass voice added to the confusion caused by the dust and smoke, the yelling, and the thunderous echoes of gunshots in the pass. The old cowman swore at those two out in the roadway, who were trading lead with his riders. Finally, in an excess of wrathful excitement, he sprang out into full sight and flung away his emptied carbine, drew his six-gun, and began an inexorable advance toward the exposed roadway.

MacCallister saw Thorne's uninjured hireling swing to blast out at DeFore, and he dropped that man with any one of three rapid shots he threw at him.

Then, under the barrage of bullets, Ray Thorne finally fell. He rolled over, tried to get up, succeeded in only getting up onto all fours. He hung there as DeFore covered the last fifty feet, stooped over him, and put his cocked pistol to the gunman's temple.

Klinger cried out. So did MacCallister. DeFore froze. For an interminable moment the diminishing life of Ray Thorne hung in the breathless balance. But DeFore didn't pull the trigger. He straightened up, eased off the hammer, and slowly, almost reluctantly, holstered his six-gun.

Ethan went over to John, who was dabbing at blood on his face from those flying, razor-sharp particles of stone.

"You all right?" he asked.

"Yeah, some rock fragments hit me with all the shooting, not Thorne's slug. Come on, let's get out there before DeFore changes his mind."

They shuffled down to the roadway, and as they did so Clem Whipple, craning over his shoulder, recognized the two lawmen and leaned back to halt his stage. It hadn't stopped moving before Charles Mather, holding his ridiculous little pearl-handled pistol, tumbled out, almost lost his balance, and came staggering over where six armed men were standing over Thorne. Behind Mather came the two mine guards, and finally the last man to hasten over was Clem, looking very pale.

MacCallister knelt, eased Thorne back over, and lifted his head. DeFore, standing over Thorne, looked as savage and as unrelenting as death itself. Mather came up, shouldered through the DeFore cowboys and would have also shouldered aside big, raw-boned old Richard DeFore, except that the cowman wouldn't give. Instead, he stood his ground and swung his smoky gaze at Mather, glaring.

"Who the hell are you?" he growled.

"Charles Mather, an officer of the stage line. Who are you?"

DeFore stepped back, ran a cold look down Mather and up again, then said coldly: "I'm Richard DeFore. That mean anything to you?"

Mather's eyes sprang wide open. He and DeFore seemed to forget entirely about Thorne and the others as they measured and assessed one another.

The sheriff's question brought the attention of the two men back to Thorne.

"Why didn't you throw down your guns?" Klinger asked Thorne. "You didn't have a chance, and you knew it."

The gunfighter rolled dimming eyes over at Klinger, then at MacCallister as he said faintly: "For seventy thousand, Sheriff, a man will take a chance . . . even if it's a poor one."

Mather peered down at Thorne, and rapped out: "Thorne, you lied to me. You lied to me all through this, didn't you?"

"Sure," the gunfighter answered, a look of scorn washing over his face. "Sure I lied, fat man. What of it?"

Mather started to speak, checked himself, and along with the others now crowding around, watched Thorne's chest fall in, watched his eyes glaze, watched his head go slack upon MacCallister's arm.

It was Klinger who ordered: "Clem, go fetch the coach."

Ethan stood up, gazed around, saying to DeFore: "How about you and your boys going back for the horses . . . all of them, Dick? We'll tie the dead ones across their saddles and take Thorne back with us."

DeFore nodded. He took one last look at the gunfighter and then grimly walked away, followed by his men.

Ethan let them get beyond earshot before he turned to Charles Mather to say: "Mather, you made one bad mistake."

"Yes, I realize that now. Thorne. I'm sorry, Deputy. I'm sorry for all the things I said as well."

"You going to make another one, Mather?"

The fat man's florid face looked somewhat offended. "What do you mean?"

"With Richard DeFore. He'll dedicate Cheyenne Pass . . . let it become a regular roadway. But there are some conditions attached to that."

Mather spread both his hands out, palms up. "Anything," he said. "Anything at all, Deputy."

"Closed land on both sides of the road, a turnout to be built below the top out, no passengers to be let out in the pass . . . and your word that you'll respect his rights."

"I'll give you my word to those terms, Sher- . . . Deputy . . ."—his eyes shifted over to Klinger— "and to you, Sheriff."

Klinger said dryly: "Give your word to him, Mister Mather, not us, and maybe you'd better give it to Mister DeFore in writing."

"Certainly, Sheriff, certainly. I have paper and pen in my valise on the coach. I'll write him out an agreement right now. And, Sheriff . . . I apologize again."

"Seems like some men got to live through a battle before they get any sense," John said. "Best get your satchel and write up that agreement now. DeFore'll be back in a few minutes."

Mather hustled over to the coach accompanied by the two mine guards. They halted where Clem was tooling their coach back into the roadway heading toward the mouth of the pass.

MacCallister looked around with a squint as DeFore came walking back, leading their animals as well as the horses belonging to Thorne's would-be outlaw crew.

"Son," Ethan said to John. "You're exactly what I thought you were . . . a damned good lawman." He swung back and smiled. "Now suppose we get back to town and see if maybe we can't talk your wife . . . my daughter . . . into cooking us up a big breakfast. I'm hungry enough to eat a steer, horns and all."

They retrieved their mounts from DeFore,

staying clear as Charles Mather took a long look over at Richard DeFore, then walked out where the old cowman was grimly standing with his horse, watching his riders lash the dead renegades across their saddles.

Neither MacCallister nor Klinger could hear what those two said but they saw them shake hands. They also saw DeFore accept a piece of paper from Charles Mather and pinch up his face as he laboriously read what Mather had written. And finally, they saw the rugged old cowman incline his head and once more shake Mather's hand.

Clem, high atop his seat, called down that he was ready to head back, so both the lawmen mounted. When all were ready and settled, they eased out heading northward back up the road toward Winchester.

When the town finally came into sight, MacCallister looked over and said to his son-in-law: "You know, in the last week or so you've gotten ten years of experience all jammed up into a few days. I admit I had my doubts from the start how this would affect you as it played out. But you came through fine, and I doubt like the devil if anything like this will come up again for another ten years."

John Klinger smiled. "Ethan, if you're still with me when it comes the next time, I won't care."

ABOUT THE AUTHOR

Lauran Paine, under his own name and various pseudonyms, has written over a thousand books, and was born in Duluth, Minnesota. His family moved to California when he was at a young age and his apprenticeship as a Western writer came about through the years he spent in the livestock trade, rodeos, and even motion pictures where he served as an extra because of his expert horsemanship in several films starring movie cowboy Johnny Mack Brown. In the late 1930s, Paine trapped wild horses in northern Arizona and, for a time, even worked as a professional farrier. Paine came to know the Old West through the eyes of many who had been born in the 19th Century, and he learned that Western life had been very different from the way it was portrayed on the screen. "I knew men who had killed other men," he later recalled. "But they were the exceptions. Prior to and during the Depression, people were just too busy eking out an existence to indulge in Saturday-night brawls." He served in the U.S. Navy in the Second World War and began writing for Western pulp magazines following his discharge. It is interesting to note that his earliest novels were published in the British market and he soon had as strong a following in that country as in the United States. Paine's Western fiction is characterized by strong plots, authenticity, an apparently effortless ability to construct situation and character, and a preference for building his stories upon a solid foundation of historical fact. *Adobe Empire* (1956), one of his best novels, is a fictionalized account of the last twenty years in the life of trader William Bent and, in an off-trail way, has a melancholy, bittersweet texture that is not easily forgotten. In later novels like *The White Bird* (1997) and *Cache Cañon* (1998), he showed that the special magic and power of his stories and characters had only matured along with his basic themes of changing times, changing attitudes, learning from experience, respecting Nature, and the yearning for a simpler, more moderate way of life.

| Books are produced in the United States using U.S.-based materials | Books are printed using a revolutionary new process called THINKtech™ that lowers energy usage by 70% and increases overall quality | Books are durable and flexible because of Smyth-sewing | Paper is sourced using environmentally responsible foresting methods and the paper is acid-free |

Center Point Large Print
600 Brooks Road / PO Box 1
Thorndike, ME 04986-0001 USA

(207) 568-3717

US & Canada:
1 800 929-9108
www.centerpointlargeprint.com